Star
Struck
Initiation

Ri'chard J. Caldwell

Back cover photo taken by Prestige Portraits
www.prestigeportraits.com

ISBN: 978-0-578-00173-9

Published by MoMas Press

Printed in the United States of America.

Star Struck
Initiation

-For my Mom and my friends in San Antonio and Mesquite.
Thanks for believing in me.

Contents

Warning

Be sure to read "The Prologue" before you start chapter 1. If you skip the prologue, you will not understand the story.

Thank you.

The Prologue

The flames blazed uncontrollably into the night sky, lining it with crimson streaks of light. A pre-colonial estate was ablaze in the hills. Firefighters rushed feverishly to extinguish the home. It was presumed empty, its occupants on vacation, completely oblivious to the damage being done to their property. News reporters were at the front gate of the mansion, setting up to cover the story of the fire that started on its own. Concerned neighbors crowded around them, desperately hoping that their friends weren't in the building that was being charbroiled.

Inside, pillars of smoke bellowed endlessly throughout the house. The walls were covered from floor to ceiling in flames, and there I was right in the middle of it all, holding a terrified feline with its claws digging into my arms. (What a great way to spend an evening, huh?) The flames rose higher and the smoke grew thicker as I searched, frantically, for an exit. There was only one. One of the support beams cracked and fell inches away from Mr. Jinxie (the cat) and me. Unfortunately, that exact beam had just barricaded the only hope of survival.

How do I get myself into these things? I thought. In actuality, I knew how; my mouth constantly writes checks that I can't cash. This no longer felt like a good idea. I was about to die, and this whole thing could have been avoided if I had just told the phalanx that I didn't have my abilities yet. They might have understood, but none of it mattered now. The flames crept closer and closer to us. The heat became unbearable and the air was so thin that I was getting light headed. *This is the end*, I thought.

You know how supposedly when you're about to die, your whole life flashes before your eyes? Well, that was slightly true for me. I flashed back to the one event that caused my whole life to change: The Meteor Shower. Six months ago, my science class went to the planetarium to witness the meteor shower, blissfully unaware of the chaos and destruction that the shower would bring. This is where my new life began.

Chapter 1

"Action"

Action: An exertion of power or force.

It was 6:45 a.m.; the sun had just begun to peek over the hills, when my alarm clock alerted me that it was time to get up. I fumbled around, recklessly, in search of the snooze button (which is very difficult to do with your eyes closed.) The button was eventually found and I sluggishly arose from my slumber.

"What day is it?" I asked aloud.

I could never remember what day it was, or even where I was, after I awoke from a great dream. This particular one was the best I've had in awhile, but its meaning eluded me.

In this dream, there was a gardener with five seeds of an unknown origin. I could not make out the gardener's facial features because his face was veiled in a blinding, white light. The faceless gardener knelt down to a patch of fresh soil. Using only his hands he dug five evenly spaced holes. In each hole, he placed one seed and then reburied the hole. The faceless gardener dusted himself off and went to fetch a water pail. A few yards away, there was another gardener, whose face was also concealed. The only difference was that this gardener was shrouded in darkness. He, too, had planted five seeds evenly apart from each other and had already begun watering his seeds.

The light gardener had come back to his plot of land and was also watering the seeds. Both gardeners finished watering and receded from the garden. Somehow, time accelerated rapidly and the seeds grew. The plants on both sides climbed higher and higher into the air, except for one seed. One of the light gardener's seeds wasn't moving. The dark gardener seemed to enjoy this because he cackled slightly. Higher and higher, the plants grew, but the one seed still didn't move. The dark gardener laughed a bit harder at this point. After the plants had ceased vertical growth, they moved horizontally.

I'm not kidding; the plants began to grow sideways towards each other. Within seconds, the plants were directly in front of one another. Suddenly, (and this is the part where things got strange) the dark plants coiled around the light plants, slowly suffocating them. I realized that without the fifth light plant, the dark plants outnumbered them. I glanced over at the light gardener to see if he was worried, but it was hard to tell (his face was still veiled). I did see him, however, calmly glide over to the dormant seed's location, cover it in dried brush and lit the brush on fire. I wondered why he would do something like that and moments later I got my answer.

I don't understand how, but the flames had awakened the sleeping pod. A vibrant plant came bursting from the pile of burning compost. I, then, realized that the fire was a catalyst for this plant, causing it to grow at an exponential rate. It easily caught up the other plants, even surpassing them in height. I think the dark plants noticed this and released their death grip on the light plants. The dark plants regrouped in a line formation, as did the light plants. It was an old fashioned standoff, Good VS. Evil. After what felt like ages, the dark plants broke the silence by launching dangerous looking vines towards the good plants, who countered with the same attack. Just before the blows hit, I woke up.

I really wished I knew how this dream ended, because I felt that this was foretelling something. Something horrible. I let out an elongated yawn and swung my feet over the bed to stand up. I stood up far too rapidly, because I fell back down almost immediately. I tried again to stand and was successful. I walked, shakily, to my bedroom window and opened it. Inhaling deeply the crisp, semi-humid San Antonio air, I thought *Business as usual.* Was it impossible for me to be any more wrong? Looking back on it, I seriously doubt that.

Exhaling, I closed the window and headed towards my bathroom, mentally going through my checklist: Get up, shower, get dressed, and go to school. Rarely did I have time to grab breakfast and when I did, it wasn't appreciated. Then again, cramming toast and juice down your throat never really counted as breakfast. Something I did look forward to in the morning was the perfect shower. Although it took years to fine-tune, my shower ran perfect water. Not too hot, not too cold.

After my soothing shower, I dried off and looked in the mirror. I wiped the steam from the glass to get a better look. My skin was pretty dark that morning. But then again, I was always dark. If you're black and you live in South Texas, you're kinda asking for it. My eyes were a dark brown, almost black. I'm about 5'10 and really skinny for my age. I ran my tongue over my teeth and then through the gap in my two front teeth. I hate my gap so much but I'm learning to live with it. I brushed my mini afro, left the bathroom and scavenged for something to wear. On my bed, I noticed a pair of blue jeans with a note attached to them.

Must be from mom, I deducted. She had brought them in while I was in the shower. The note read:

Pork chop,
    David bought you some new jeans. I hope you like them.
Love, Mommy.

Even though I was almost sixteen, my mom still insisted she be called Mommy. She also loved calling me pork chop, which wasn't the greatest of nicknames. Especially since it had nothing to do with my actual name. My name is Franklin J. Lamberg. I asked her once about the name and she responded: "I'd call you my little lamb chop, if we both didn't hate them with a passion." It was a good explanation.

David, the new guy. My mom's new boyfriend, who constantly tried to impress me but always failed miserably. Come to think of it, most of my mom's past boyfriends couldn't impress me. I had always thought that each guy had nothing to offer my mom and I. As I look back on it now, maybe the true reason I was never impressed is because I knew my dad. I grew up with my dad around for eleven years, but one day, he fell overboard while on a cruise line. However, they never recovered a body, so I had hoped that, somehow, he was still alive and would come back. My hopes stayed that way until my mom started dating again two years later. I did protest for a while, but eventually I just abandoned all hope. I wanted my mom to be happy, and a presumed dead person couldn't do that. At least, I hoped not.

I lifted the jeans off the bed and tried them on. They fit as well as a circus tent. I quickly removed and discarded the jeans, making my way over to the closet.

Amidst rummaging my wardrobe, I glanced up at the clock. It appeared to be 8:15 a.m. *Crap*, I thought. *I'm gonna miss the bus.* (Although I had my own car, I couldn't "legally" drive it yet.) So, after snatching the nearest pair of jeans and a shirt, I set out for school. In my hurried state, I almost plummeted down the stairs. Outside, there was a red headed person with dark green eyes, standing at about 5'8, waiting for me. His hair was on the longish side, almost completely covering his eyes. He had an average body type; you could tell he frequented the gym from time to time. I saw him out there as soon as I opened the front door.

"You're gonna make us late!" he said angrily, though I wasn't paying any attention to him.

Today, for some unknown reason, his freckles had my focus. They seemed to go on for days. *Had there always been so many*? I wondered.

"Flames," he said, "snap out of it."

Flames: it's what my friends called me. Now this nickname made much more sense. By taking the first letter of my first name and the first three letters of my last name, "Flam" was born. My peers, who thought flam didn't mean anything, took it one step further. When they added the "es", they had created a new identity for me.

Flames became my alter ego. The person that majority of my friends knew and who I really was were completely opposite. Perhaps the only person on earth that knew both sides of me was standing directly in front of me. Derrick McGuire had been my best friend since before I could remember. Growing up, we were inseparable. Ireland and Jamaica united by the two of us. Truthfully, neither one of us have accents that would tell where we are from. Actually, no one would know unless they were told.

"As fun as this is, I kinda wanted to see the shooting stars." Derrick announced.

I dusted myself off and headed to the bus with derrick.

"You know," I began telling him, "They're not really stars at all, but space rocks that have broken apart from larger ones."

This was me. I was a brainiac. I studied for tests, even though I told everyone that I didn't. I read books, but told people I was a television addict. I acted like an average teenager, when I was really everything but.

Peering upward at the sky, you wouldn't have thought that in less than four hours, meteor fragments would penetrate the earth's atmosphere and change the lives of dozens of people. I wonder, as I'm standing here in this inferno, what would my life be like if I had missed the school bus. Would I be risking my life for a petrified cat inside of hell's kitchen, or would I be at home, studying for my SAT's?

The bus arrived late, as usual, to pick us up. Derrick and I, along with the rest of the bus stop, loaded routinely on to the bus. Our bus is always a little overcrowded, which caused us to create a system. Everyone in the back of the bus (the cool section) had a seat to save for someone else. That way, no matter when you got on the bus, your seat was waiting.

The one thing that made our bus special was the people. On this bus was the greatest bunch of people you could ever meet. There is a multitude of people that I could introduce you to, but only four of them play a crucial role in the events to come: Staci Peterson, Danny Moore, Hannah Hernandez, and Curtis Burray.

Staci had pale skin and wore black eyeliner which intensified the brightness of her brown eyes. She was only 5'6 but when she wore her dark hair in a ponytail (which she did often) she seemed taller. Staci loved magic tricks. She was always great with a deck of cards. There had even been a few instances where everyone thought her tricks were real.

"Slide of hand," she would say. "It's all about the slide of hand."

Danny was 5'6 and, compared to Staci, he was really tan. With his cream colored skin, bluish green eyes, dark brown, shaggy hair, athletic build, and a scar over his right eyebrow, Danny was something of a heartthrob among the ladies but he never let it go to his head. Instead, Danny was the bus prankster. He would try anything to make you laugh: impersonations, sex jokes, even politics. Some of his impersonations were dead-on, too. However, not all of Danny's remarks bode well for him. There was one incident where Danny said: "Hey, you wanna hear a joke...Women's rights." The girls of the bus left him with a few bruises for that one.

Hannah and Curt were dating. They had been for a few weeks now. Hannah was the silent type. She was Hispanic with very light brown eyes and hair. When Hannah's hair wasn't flowing freely, she had it up in two ponytails. Hannah was only 5'5 and she had an exceptionally lean figure. She never really would contribute to the bus conversations and, at times, it was like she wasn't even there.

Curt, the complete opposite of Hannah, was very talkative. He was great at comforting people in pain. Although he was from South Korea originally, living in San Antonio has given Curt such a tan that he looked Mexican. He had hazel eyes and had semi-long black hair but he was usually seen sporting a fauxhawk. The Cross Country coaches didn't like his hair but they couldn't say anything; he was one of the best on the team. He also kinda towered over Hannah, being 4 inches taller than her. This teen had advice on everything under the sun. He also had the answer to almost any question, before it was asked. There were a few moments when I was sure Curt could read minds. I understood why the two were dating, they completed each other.

As I strolled back to my usual seat, I picked up on today's bus discussion. It seemed that everyone was buzzing over the meteor shower. Derrick and I took our seats and the bus door squeaked to a close. The bus driver, Bryan, shifted gears and took off. There we were, on a yellow school bus, cascading toward the unknown.

Chapter 2

"Realization"

Realization: The act of grasping or understanding clearly.

The element of surprise. Throughout history, many battles and wars have had their outcomes altered by surprises. The Trojan horse, for example, was one of the greatest of all time. Apparently, the meteor had this specific element on its side.

I couldn't explain why, but I was suddenly compelled to listen to the radio. Reaching into my backpack, I retrieved my MP3 player and searched for the radio feature. I located it quite easily, but there wasn't music playing. A public broadcast, about the meteor shower, had just commenced.

"Due to recent developments discovered by NASA," The DJ began, "All meteor watches have been deemed pointless. According to NASA's representatives, there is no longer a meteor to watch. They say the meteor became a threat to national security when it flew dangerously close to earth."

A threat to the nation's security? What happened to the meteors? I wondered. As if responding, the DJ continued the broadcast.

"At precisely 6:45 a.m., a U.S. missile made contact with the meteor. It shattered on impact and its remains dispersed back into space."

The DJ finished the announcement and the station returned to the music.

Utter shock and disappointment coursed through my veins. How could NASA do that? Meteors, large enough to see, only came around every hundred years or so. Had this really happened? Had the meteor of my generation really been destroyed by nervous astronauts? I, then, thought about the time that all of this occurred. 6:45 a.m.? That's the exact time my dream concluded…could there be a correlation? Perhaps, or maybe I was overanalyzing the situation. After all, I have been known to do that.

Poking my head out the window, I looked up at the sky. There had not been a cloud in the sky that day. It had been perfect weather conditions to witness the shower.

"Gone? Is it really gone? Is today gonna be yet another uneventful day?" I asked, rhetorically.

Looking back on that day, in light of my present situation, I can't help but laugh at myself. I had wanted, so badly, to have an adventure. I desired to break away from the mundane, white bread life I had to live and do something exciting. The phrase, "Be careful what you wish for," has never really hit home before now. I had wished for change, and got it…in a big way.

NASA believed they had saved the world from a deadly meteor. At that very moment, they were probably drinking champagne in celebration. They assumed that the meteor pieces had retreated into the vast reaches of space. NASA had no idea how wrong they truly were. It appeared that the meteor shower was closer to Earth than they estimated. It seemed that, directly after the explosion, the rock did diverge into hundreds of tiny pieces, but they didn't return to space.

The earth's gravitational pull had acted as a vacuum, sucking each and every shard of debris into the atmosphere. Due to the size of the pieces, they snuck past NASA's radars undetected. Gone? I wish. No, they were still coming, even sooner than originally expected. I reeled my head back into the vehicle, and sat there, gloomily, mentally preparing for the day ahead.

The usual bus route seemed so redundant. Day in and day out, we passed the usual burger joint, dollar store, and gas station. Preceding them, the same old bank, grocery store, and movie rental place plagued my vision. Twenty stoplights, twelve miles, and six hundred and forty-seven irritating road bumps later, we pulled into the Lincoln parking lot. Abraham Lincoln High School had been there for centuries, but was recently remodeled a few years back. The bus came to a grinding halt, and students spewed out of it. As I exited, I noticed the turf sidewalks. Had they always been maroon? I felt like a blind person, granted his sight once again.

Xavier Gonzalez, the bus mute, gave me an innocent shove as he passed me. Breaking my trance, I lifted my head and smirked at him. X was Mexican although his skin was really light. He had green eyes and black hair that was cut so low that he looked bald from a distance. He never talked to anyone on the bus, but me. Everyone had thought Xavier was mute, because every time they would talk to him, he would just give them a blank stare. In fact, no one, besides me, had ever really heard him speak.

I was the only person that called Xavier "X". (Honesty, I was probably the only person who knew X's full name.) Standing at about 5'7, X was three inches shorter than me, but a million times faster, which is why he ran track and had the body of a sprinter. In reality, Xavier was nowhere near being a mute; he just chose not to answer the "stupid" questions that he was asked.

Derrick, explaining that he had track practice, left for the recreational center, so I jogged to catch X.

"You know it's still coming, right?" Xavier said to me before I had reached him.

"What?" I asked in confusion.

"The meteor's fragments, they're still coming." He replied.

"Intuition?" I asked

"Intuition." He responded.

One very important fact that should be known about X, he's extremely intuitive. He has been that way as long as I've known him. We met in the 2nd grade. It was the first day of school; everyone was present and accounted for, except the teacher. No one knew where he was, that is no one but X. He was new to the state, but this didn't stop him from approaching me. Xavier didn't speak much back then either, but what he did say still amazes me.

"Mr. Brown's engine has flooded. That is why he is tardy."

I figured Xavier was just making conversation, but moments later; the teacher came into the class.

He introduced himself as Mr. Brown and apologized for being late. He complained that he had a flooded engine and was forced to take a cab. After noticing our blank expression, he decided to teach us what an engine was. I was astonished. I looked to Xavier, who turned to me and smiled. How did this new kid know that Mr. Brown's engine had flooded? Why did he tell me? How did he know what an engine was? Each of these questions darted through my mind that day. There was one fact that I knew for sure: This was the coolest, smartest kid I had ever met. I had to be friends with him.

"Hi, my name is Franklin, what's yours?"

Xavier pushed the hair from his eyes and said, "My name is Xavier."

As a second grader, my memory span was the same size as that of a goldfish.

So, naturally, I was terrible at remembering names.

"Xavier," I started, "That starts with an X, right?"

Xavier nodded in agreement.

"That's kinda hard to remember, I'm gonna call you X, ok?" I asked.

"Um, ok." X replied. Since then, X and I have been great friends. Something I've learned about Xavier: his intuition was never wrong. If X said there would be a pop quiz in geometry, I started studying.

Hearing X say that the asteroid shards were still coming brightened my temperament. Nothing could ruin my day, not even the looming penitentiary-like learning establishment. Lincoln High was a massive school, the second largest in the district. With its titanium gates and watchtower-like structures, Lincoln was constantly mistaken for a correctional facility. Our school gave one a sense of smallness. Shaking off this sensation, X and I passed under the archway towards homeroom.

"Hey, X," I began, "How are we gonna see the shower if the trip has been cancelled?"

Xavier stopped moving and faced me.

"They've rescheduled the class to go to the park and just spend all day there." Xavier paused, and then continued. "Everything is about to change, Flames. Something tragic is going to happen by day's end. All of these events revolve around the meteor fragments."

This statement didn't just rain on my parade, it soaked the whole festival. Something tragic? I hadn't known it then, but, as always, Xavier was right on the money.

We resumed our walking pace, when I accidentally grazed the flagpole, causing a surprisingly powerful static discharge. I yelped in pain. This always happened to me. At the most inopportune times, I would emit static shock. In several incidents, I've, inadvertently, started miniature fires. I patted out my smoking sleeve, while X tried to stifle his laughter. He never laughed much; in fact, these random combustions were the only things that tickled him. I sighed in relief after I stopped steaming, then continued with X on to class.

Xavier and I entered the classroom mere moments before the bell sounded. Danny, Staci, Hannah, and Curt were already seated, so we joined them. Grabbing the nearest available seats, we placed our backpacks down and prepared to work. We all were anxious to learn what awaited us today. A pale man, by the name of Mr. Protium, came silently into the room. He resembled a beanstalk and his lime green suit, complete with matching shoes, didn't help.

He spoke in a nasally, monotone voice when he told us the news.

"Students," He started, "I assume you have heard that the meteor has been eliminated. So, I have been informed that, as a substitute, we will venture to the unknown area of...Lincoln Memorial Park."

Lincoln Park? It's ironic, NASA tried to prevent the asteroid from coming to us, but now, we were going to it. Lincoln Park would come to be known as the place affected hardest by the meteor shards, but who could have predicted that our science class would end up in the eye of the storm? Oh, right, X could've and he did.

I leaned over to X and whispered, "X, when you said that everything was gonna change and that something tragic would happen before the end of the day, exactly when will all of this start?"

Xavier seemed to be collecting his thoughts, and then he turned to answer me. I have to admit, what I saw in X's expression frightened me. His face had flushed dead white; my good friend was genuinely spooked. Xavier's lips trembled as he attempted to answer my question. The words that came from his mouth had the most ominous tone I had ever heard in my life.

"Flames," He said, "All that I have foretold...has already begun."

Chapter 3

"Transformation"

Transformation: To change in form, appearance or structure.

The metamorphic phase. Caterpillars undergo this stage of life and emerge as butterflies. Blocks of clay go through this as well and come out as beautiful works of art. On that day, ten people entered the park as lumps of coal, but exited as spotless diamonds. All but one, that is. It seemed that I was unaffected by the events that occurred. Xavier had been correct once again with his premonition, something tragic had happened. By 11:59 p.m., someone would be pronounced dead.

We arrived at Lincoln Park by 11:59 a.m., but it felt later. The ride there was stale and eventless, except for Staci and Danny's confrontation. I was doodling on one of my school folders when I heard them.

"Danny! Stop touching my hair!"

Danny had been messing with Staci's ponytail for the last five minutes. He refused to leave her alone. Danny had left Staci no choice. She quickly whipped around, seized Danny by the hair, and began pulling him over her seat.

"Okay! Okay! I'll Stop!" He screamed, as she pulled harder. Danny's face blushed rose red.

"You know what? I need a picture of this." Staci said.

Going through her purse, she pulled out a camera.

"Hey Frankie," she called to me. "Could you take a picture of this?"

I grabbed the camera from her hands and was prepared to take it, when Danny freed himself from Staci's grip of death. He instantly settled back in his seat, straightened his hair, and didn't say another word the rest of the way. This was an exciting event, one that I would have normally missed. I usually didn't sit by Staci and Danny, I actually sat closer to the front, but today was different. This day, I witnessed the failure of our system. There had been someone in my seat when I boarded the bus: A girl. It wasn't just any girl; it was Kimberly Johnson.

Kim Johnson was the most hated person at Lincoln - with good reason. She was originally from our sister school, George Washington High School. Washington was where all the "rich" kids went to school. One day, however, the principal of Washington High began getting complaints of overcrowding at their precious school. So, in a unanimous decision, the school board ruled that Washington should be capped out. This forced hundreds of their students to relocate within the district. Kim, being from Washington, figured she was automatically better than us. She was condescending, annoying, and self-centered; basically, Kim was a huge witch with a capital B.

Of all the seats on the bus, she chose mine to steal. Kim hadn't known it then, but she may have accidentally saved my life.

"What are you doing in my seat, Kim Jong Il?" I asked irately.

Everyone called Kim that because of her dictator-like personality, even though she was clearly Indian.

She swung her jet-black hair and answered, "Excuse me?" in a snobbish tone. "There are, like, a million seats on this piece of tin foil...go find one."

With this, Kim rolled her eyes and turned away.

At that very moment, I sincerely desired to beat her with a toaster, but decided against it. I had remembered that I didn't hit girls (no matter how stuck-up) and that I didn't have a toaster to beat her with. Realizing that I would be fighting a losing battle, I gave up and continued to the latter part of the bus. I grabbed the nearest seat with my friend/rival Jared Jones, and that's where I was when Danny was emasculated.

Jared had been my friend since the 9th grade. He was Mexican but you wouldn't be able to tell by looking at him. He had really light skin and dark brown eyes which could barely be seen since he squinted so much. And, because of these features, as well as his black, bowl-cut hair, many people confused him for Asian. Another strange characteristic about Jared was that he had oddly large lips. No one knew why. He just did.

Anyway, Jared and I have been rivals long before we were friends. We had been competing with each other since-I'd say-about 5th grade. Back then I was the undefeated champ in all things remotely related to school. Then Jared moved here and the balance shifted.

A few weeks after he came, we had our year-end exam. Being the cocky kid that I was at that age, I was sure that I would pass it with flying colors. I did ace that test, but Jared beat me. I was devastated. I had never lost. *never!* Some random kid came along and knocked me off my pedestal. I quickly went from destroyed to pissed. Then from pissed to determined. I had to be on top again. Or so I thought.

For the next few years, I would beat Jared at one thing, but then he'd come back with another. It was a never-ending cycle. I couldn't understand it. I never had to work hard to be the best; it would just happen that way. We were too evenly matched. Neither of us would back down. At the beginning of 9th grade, our rivalry became friendly instead of bloody.

Jared was always the calm one. He usually had a level head and a plan. Honestly, we were like fire and water: complete opposites. For me, when a problem struck, I struck back. No plan, just willpower. I never planned things too far out. This, in my opinion, is part of the reason that I'm in this flaming furnace.

Jared was 5'10, just like me. Come to think of it, most of my friends were around that height. Except for X, of course. And Sarita. *oh!* I almost forgot about Sarita. She's kinda important too.

I had a crush on Sarita Cruise in the 3rd grade. I told her about it that year, on Valentine's Day. She hit me with her bag of candy and that was the end of that. She could have her moods at times.

Sarita was about 5'3, with caramel skin and jet black braids that stretched down her back. She wore glasses with thick lenses that made her dark brown eyes look larger than they actually were. For the most part, Sarita's cool. She can be nurturing, almost mother-like, when you feel sick or sad. Sarita also had a wicked green thumb. Anything that she planted would grow to enormous sizes and heights. That day, she sat in front of Jared and I.

"Suicidal Sammy has struck again." Sarita said, as she turned to face us.

Suicidal Sammy was the neighborhood cat who-you guessed it–was suicidal. Or so we said. His real name is Mr. Jinxie and, for the two years that he has been on this earth, he has pulled various stunts that appear to be suicide related. No one ever understood why. My mom used to say he was just creative. I'm pretty sure that was her nice way of saying that he was stupid. Suicidal Sammy's owner was one of the richest men in the city.

The owner's name is unimportant; what is important is where he lived. Suicidal Sammy's owner lived in a very large, very old mansion on the highest of the rolling hills. Last time I checked, it was on fire. Looking around at these torched paintings and flaming coaches, it seems pretty nice in here. Except for the whole "house on fire, I'm gonna die" thing. I honesty wouldn't be surprised if Suicidal Sammy started this fire. Surely, if we survive this, Suicidal Sammy won't be so suicidal.

"Are you serious?" Jared asked.

I sighed, "What did he do this time?" I asked.

Holding back giggles, Sarita explained how yesterday, he walked into the street (in front of a car) and laid down. We all shared a laugh this.

"That cat is gonna..."

Jared was interrupted by a high-pitched screech. It was Kim.

"Like Ow! Who did that?!" She screamed and turned to face us.

There was complete silence. No one was paying attention to her. Maybe we should have. Was it possible that Kim's demise could have been averted? I honesty don't know. I do, however, know what Kim had mistaken for a childish antic turned out to be the one thing that took her life.

Kim's window had been open when it happened. The first wave of fragments had just pierced the sky. They, for the most part, had been heading to the same location: Lincoln Park. All but two: these two separated from the group and began to accelerate. The first chunk crashed harmlessly into the seemingly empty Amy Caster community swimming pool, but the second one seemed to have a mind of its own.

The second one had headed towards the bus that we were on. Faster and faster it descended, gaining on the bus in no time flat. The fragment entered Kim's open window perfectly and penetrated her ear. It lodged itself in her brain and sent out a surge of electricity. This is what caused Kim to scream.

When no one answered her question, Kim gave up and turned back around in her seat.

"What an attention whore!" Jayden exclaimed to Sarita.

"Jayden!" Sarita said in a humorous manner.

Jayden usually spoke her mind. I think that's what I liked about her. Actually, I think that's what everyone liked about her. She always says what most people are afraid to say.

She was a really cool person if you took the time to get to know her. Jayden had brown everything: brown hair, brown eyes and brown skin. And, to put it simply, she was curvy (in a good way) so guys gave her a lot of attention. Although she's only 5'4, don't let Jayden's size fool you; she's feisty.

It's hard not to like Jayden. Anything that you're interested in, she was too. If you like skateboarding, so does she. If you like dark poetry, she's been writing that for years. Anything that you can think of, Jayden liked it or at least had tried to like it. It was like she'd copy people's experiences and hobbies; like a chameleon. She could adapt to almost any situation. Yeah, this Puerto Rican girl could do everything - except get along with Kim. They had been mortal enemies since Kim tore the head off of Jayden's doll in the 1st grade. Even after all these years, Kim had never apologized and Jayden had never forgiven her.

I had settled back in my seat and looked out the window, when I realized where we were. The bus was pulling into the parking lot in front of Lincoln Park. Overhead, the blanket of meteorites loomed menacingly and began to lose altitude rapidly. The bus came to a full stop and we all filed out.

Jared and I had just gotten off when a tiny pebble hit him in the back of the head.

"Ow. What was that?" He asked.

We both looked down and saw the culprit.

"Hm," Jared said, "I guess the meteor shower is still coming after all."

I instantly flashed back to earlier that day. *X said the shower was still coming and it is,* I thought. *That's not surprising. X is always right. But he also said everything would change. What did he mean?* I started imagining the possibilities and shuttered.

"NASA was wrong," Jared said, "The meteor shower is still coming. I hope it isn't to broken up to see."

I agreed listlessly and we left for the field.

I guess the shower is still coming after all. Neither of us knew it then, but this was the greatest understatement of all time.

Chapter 4

"Mutation"

Mutation: an inherited physical or biochemical change in one's

genetic material.

There is no better word for what occurred that day. We were mutated. The irony of it all was that no one knew what was happening until it was too late.

By the time my science class had unloaded off the bus, hundreds of meteorite shards had been scattered across the park. It was eerily desolate there. In fact, we were the only people at Lincoln Park.

The buses swiftly drove off and I regrouped with my friends. Jared, Sarita, Staci, Danny, Xavier, Jayden, Hannah, Curt, Derrick, and I were about to decide what to do, when Laura and Chris walked up.

Laura Evergreen and Chris Flores had been dating since I set them up in the 8th grade. These two were truly an odd couple. Laura, with her blonde hair and tiny frame, was a soft, somewhat passive person. Standing at a mere 5'5 with a soft, oval face, and light brown eyes, Laura was very affectionate and kind; basically, everything that Chris wasn't.

Chris Flores was a big, sturdy-looking guy who lived, breathed, ate and worshipped soccer. This Mexico native had hazel eyes and short, black hair that he gelled forward on a daily basis. Not to say Chris was the stereotypical jock, but...well, he was. It kinda looked like he was on steroids. Chris was huge. He was 5'11 and had bulging arms with sickly veins popping out of them and bulging legs that were the same as his arms. Now, one would think that a guy this big wouldn't have problems with people messing with him, but this was high school: *no one* was safe. Actually, on a daily basis, Chris was accused of being gay. No one really believed he was, but he had brought this on himself.

At the beginning of the year, in our history class, Mr. Drymore was going around the room asking what everyone had done over the weekend. Each person answered with miscellaneous things like going to the movies or babysitting. But when Mr. Drymore came to Chris, however, it was a much different story. Chris started to explain about a party he had gone to. He explained that, at the party, there were a lot of girls, but only a few boys.

Mr. Drymore suddenly cut Chris off by saying, "You say that like it's a *bad* thing. Is there something you would like to admit to the class? About your sexual preferences, perhaps?"

The class erupted with laughter at this. And, instead of standing up for himself, Chris just crouched down in his seat and took the criticism as fact. This fueled everyone to call him gay.

"Hey, guys." Said Laura weakly.

She always spoke quietly like this; like a whisper in the wind. It's something that she and Hannah shared.

"Hey, Wash." We all replied back.

Everyone called Laura this because she was supposed to attend Washington high, until it was capped out. We all decided that saying wash was much easier to say than Washington.

Chris grunted deeply to make his presence known. Jared turned away from Laura to look at him.

"Oh hey, Liberace," Jared said, "Didn't see you there."

We all shared a giggle at this (all but Chris, that is) and parted ways. Pairing off in twos, we all ventured to different areas of the park.

Though the specifics on how it happened to each of us vary, the result was the same: pieces of meteor dissolved into our bloodstreams and changed us. Possibly forever. And, although I didn't develop like the others, I still believe I was mutated as well. Not that it matters now. Seeing as how I'm about to die a flaming death.

The story that I can depict the most vividly was my own. Jared and I had been journeying to the center of the park, near the grills when we sparked up a heated debate over pirates and ninjas.

"*What*!?" I asked in disbelief. "There's no way pirates are better than ninjas!" I retorted. "Pirates spend months on end on a boat with a bunch of guys! *and* they believe it's *bad* luck to have a girl on board! What does that tell you?" I paused to let Jared answer, but when he didn't, I continued. "I got two words for you: Butt. Sex. It's not pretty, but it's the pirate way."

I laughed hysterically at my joke until Jared silenced me.

"Really? I guess you would know *all* about the pirate way, wouldn't you, Flames? And what about ninjas and those tight black outfits? Why black? Is it…sliming? Are scary ninjas worried about their figures?" He asked rhetorically.

I didn't think it was so funny, but Jared would've begged to differ. We continued feuding like this for a while.

Up ahead of us was the picnic area. Vast amounts of rusty grills and rotting wooden tables littered the land. Under them, was half-dead grass and thriving weeds that snaked their way through the legs of the tables and grills. The trees surrounding them looked rather sickly as well. They drooped and hung solemnly everywhere, losing leaves left and right. It wasn't an impressive park. Its run-down look was part of the reason the park was so empty.

Our science teacher had started up a grill without cleaning out the pit. He had just tossed in more charcoal on what he assumed was merely old ashes, but was completely oblivious that several dozen medium-sized meteor rocks had landed in this particular grill. After wiping the sweat from his forehead, Mr. Protium doused the coals in lighter fluid and lit a match. He effortlessly dropped the match on the wet coal, which ignited a massive fire that nearly singed his eyebrows. He stumbled clumsily backwards in shock and fell. The flame emitted an enormous pillar of smoke that brought with it meteor dust particles. A brisk wind swiftly blew by, scattering the air pollution across the park. The flame died down afterward.

Looking dazed and confused, Mr. Protium lifted himself off of the ground and brushed off the dirt that had accumulated on the back of his pants. He walked back over to check on the grill and noticed the coals were white hot, but he failed to see the meteor pieces embedded within.

That was fast, he said to himself. He picked up several nearby packages of hot dogs and placed them evenly across the grill. The coals hissed, with smoke that rose and caressed each hot dog with infected air from burning charcoal and meteor rocks. As he let the sausages sizzle, Mr. Protium stepped back to admire his work.

Jared and I abruptly interrupted his train of thought. We were still arguing when we came upon him.

"Boys. Boys." He called to us in his usual unexcited voice. Our argument ceased temporarily as we both looked to see what Mr. Protium wanted. "Boys, lunch is ready." He said.

A bewildered looked appeared on our faces as we looked upon a grill that held a large amount of semi-burnt hot dogs.

"That's lunch?" I whispered to Jared, who was preparing to answer when he suddenly got an idea.

"An eating contest." He said quietly.

"Huh?" I asked.

"An eating contest," he said louder than before. "That's how we'll settle this."

I pretended to think about and then sprinted, without warning, towards the buns and condiments, with Jared inches behind. We, rapidly, fixed our plates and slammed them down on the closest table. We inhaled hot dogs at monstrous speeds, with Mr. Protium protesting in the background.

"Boys, please, don't eat so quickly. You'll get indigestion." He said.

Ignoring his warning, Jared and I continued on. One after another, until we had both consumed 10 hot dogs, respectively.

Jared and I rose from the benches for seconds, but fell back down. We both felt an odd surge of electricity inside our bodies and became violently nauseous.

"I feel...different." We both said simultaneously and then vomited into the grass.

Mr. Protium looked, disapprovingly, at us as we retched uncontrollably.

"I told you so." He said with a cocky smirk on his face, but it disappeared when he heard someone shriek.

*****

The story of Danny and Jayden was somewhat similar to my own. Jayden had left our little gathering with intention to do something exciting and Danny went with her with the intention of making Jayden fall in love with him. He had had a crush on her for months, but his feelings were seemingly unrequited. Jayden never really appeared to notice Danny that way, no matter how he tried. But this didn't discourage him.

"I'll wear her down," he would say. "We're meant to be together."

Danny and Jayden walked east, through a mini-forest and stopped in front of the tallest tree.

"Hey, Danny," said Jayden. "I bet I'll beat you to the top."

Danny rubbed his hairless chin as he thought it over. *Maybe she'll like me if I beat her up the tree*, he thought.

"*You're on!*" He exclaimed as he shot up the tree trunk.

Danny had reached the top before Jayden had even touched the bark. *Nicely done*, He thought. *Here come the accolades*.

Jayden scaled the tree at a steady pace. When she reached the peak, she sat on the branch furthest away from Danny.

"Show-off," she muttered angrily under her breath, but Danny heard it anyway.

24

He was momentarily depressed, but decided to counter with a joke; he just had to think of a good one.

Several hundred yards away, Mr. Protium was setting up a grill. He had covered the coals in lighter fluid and pulled out a match. Mr. Protium struck it and dropped it in the pit. Flames exploded from the grill instantly and a large cloud of smoke formed in the air. The cloud was soon blown towards the tree Danny and Jayden were in.

Back at the tree, Danny had decided an impression was the way to go.

"Hey, Jay," he began. "Who am I?"

He cleared his throat as Jayden turned to face him and did his impression.

"I did not…have sexual relations…with that woman."

Danny paused for Jayden's reaction. She tried to stifle her laughter, but he had done a believable impression of former president Bill Clinton. It started as a giggle, but evolved into full chuckle. This made Danny grin ear to ear and he started to laugh himself. *Yes*, he thought. *Cool points for the Dan Man.* The two were too occupied to notice the dark sphere, that contained meteor fragments, which loomed very close to them.

The smoke engulfed their tree and swallowed all the oxygen they had. Danny and Jayden were being suffocated and they started to cough and choke roughly. Their vision was dangerously blurred and they plummeted from the tree, kicking and screaming all the way down. Danny and Jayden hit the ground with a sickening thud.

Mr. Protium looked away from Jared and me vomiting when he heard their screams and saw something fall with his peripheral vision. Upon realizing that what he saw falling was some of his students, Mr. Protium freaked out and dashed frantically to their aid. He cursed under his breath. *Oh, no.* He thought. *Another lawsuit for the school if these kids are hurt. I'm so gonna get fired.*

Surprisingly enough, nothing was broken on Danny or Jayden. But they were paralyzed from the shock of the fall.

When Mr. Protium arrived, he checked their vitals and let out a sigh of relief that they were alive. Danny and Jayden experienced a jolt of electricity, and then unexplainably developed a high fever.

Suffering from delirium and fatigue, Danny turned to Jayden, who landed about a foot away, and reached for her hand. He held it as tight as he could manage.

"You ok?" he asked weakly.

"Yeah, I'm fine. Hey, Danny, I bet I'll recover from this first." She whispered.

Danny and Jayden locked eyes and smiled at each other.

Danny mustered all the strength he had left and said, "You're on."

With this, they both slipped away from consciousness.

*****

Hannah and Curt had planned to use this trip to the park as quality time together since Hannah's parents didn't want her dating and they didn't know that Curt was more than a friend.

"Hey, Curt," Hannah squeaked as they left the group.

"Yeah?" he replied.

"Do you wanna go lay on a hill and watch the clouds go by?" she asked.

Curt glanced up at the sky. There weren't any clouds. But instead of embarrassing his girlfriend, Curt gave Hannah a huge smile and kissed her.

"Sure," he said. "Sounds fun."

They searched for the nearest hill and plopped themselves on it and there they laid, side-by-side, holding hands. The two were like this for a while, until Hannah felt parched.

"Are you thirsty?" Curt asked, as if reading her mind.

"Yes, I am." She answered meekly.

"Wait here. I'll go get us something."

Hannah smiled as she watched her boyfriend run down their lumpy hill to fetch her a beverage.

Curt strolled by Mr. Protium, who was engrossed in putting charcoal in the grill. It crossed Curt's mind to tell him that he should clean out the pit first, but decided against it. *I should get the drinks first*, he thought. Curt retrieved two cups of ice and two sodas from a cooler on top of a decaying wooden table and headed back to Hannah. He climbed back up the hill to find Hannah in the same position as he left her.

"Here you go." Curt said, grinning ear to ear as he handed her the soft drink.

"Oh," she said with a tone of disappointment. "Cherry."

Hannah couldn't stand anything cherry flavored, but it was the thought that counted.

"Thank you, Curt." She smiled and accepted the can.

Curt sat back down next to her and, pushing his emo-like hair out of his eyes, poured his soda into a cup. It was when he saw the other cup still in his possession that Curt realized he had forgotten to give Hannah her cup of ice. He quickly handed it over.

"Sorry," he said, embarrassed.

He blushed and tried to hide it by holding his cup to his face, drinking from it in the process. Hannah did the same and they both laid on their backs.

In the distance, a flame ignited and smoke rose. This smoke soon moved above Hannah and Curt, toward the tree that Danny and Jayden had been in. As the black cloud passed over Hannah and Curt, hundreds of microscopic meteor particles landed in their unshielded drinks.

"Hey, look Hannah." Curt exclaimed and pointed at the blob of smoke. "I know it's not a real cloud, but it's probably the nearest thing to one as we will get." They both laughed at this, even though it wasn't a joke.

Sitting back up, Hannah took a large gulp of her con-taminated soda and Curt did so as well.

Curt suddenly frowned. "This tastes fu-" He froze in ter-ror as he watched, across the field, Danny and Jayden fall from very high branches. He saw Mr. Protium mouthing something, as he sprinted to their aid.

"Hey, I think we should go-" Curt was cut off my Hannah's agonizing scream. He turned to her, and noticed that she was shaking violently.

"*Hannah!*" He yelled. "What's wrong?!" Curt was unable to ask any more questions nor could he provide help because he, too, had begun to have seizures.

Hannah and Curt both were shocked by a burst of energy that caused their eyes to roll back into their heads. They fell backwards to the ground, and there they laid, still hand in hand, shaking terribly. This is how they were when Mr. Protium found them.

Mr. Protium had been carrying Danny and Jayden, on both of his shoulders, towards the picnic tables, when he noticed Hannah and Curt in distress. He walked as fast as he could (because he couldn't run with the extra weight) and examined the seizuring teens.

The seizures had stopped by this time, but Curt and Hannah were not moving. Mr. Protium placed Danny and Jayden by Curt and Hannah. It turned out that Mr. Protium was stronger than he looked, but not by much because he soon collapsed from exhaustion.

Mr. Protium massaged his temples and looked at the four unconscious teenagers that laid, outstretched, in front of him and the other two, vomiting their guts out, by the grills.

Mr. Protium let out a deep sigh and mumbled, "I do not get paid enough for this." And then pulled out a cell phone, calling 911.

Laura and Chris had been sitting on an isolated bench, behind some trees, talking, when Mr. Protium was setting up the grill. They were having relationship problems at the time.

"Why can't you understand how I'm feeling?!" Laura asked in an abnormally forceful tone. Chris turned away, causing the bench to creak. He seemed to be thinking.

Although Chris looked like the average jock; he wasn't. The main and possibly only difference was that Chris was smart.

Very smart, to be specific. He was perhaps one of the smartest friends I had, but he seriously lacked common sense and Chris couldn't understand girls to save his life.

"I'm sorry, Laura. It just doesn't make sense. What's so important about holding hands in public?" He asked.

Laura tensed up angrily and pursed her lips in response, but was halted by someone's scream. The couple looked around, quizzatively, for the source. Laura and Chris both gasped as they witnessed their friends propel downward from the trees and they winced as Danny and Jayden hit the ground.

Above their heads, the cloud that had just attacked Danny and Jayden, seemed to have set its sights on Chris and Laura. Its descent was sudden, but Chris saw it in time to warn Laura to hold her breath. He believed he had thought out the entire situation, but Chris forgot one minor detail: they still had their eyes open. The two were trying to see if their friends were ok. Laura could vaguely make out a figure running towards Danny and Jayden.

I wish I could see, thought Laura. And, as if complying with her wish, a mighty gust of wind blew the hazardous air past Chris and Laura, but not before the smoke had coated their eyes in a thick layer of ash. This caused them to burn, which made Chris and Laura rub their eyes instinctively, but that only made things worse. Their eyeballs began to buzz as they felt a jolt of electricity and the two lost their sight.

Chris and Laura wandered around the park, in anguish, for a while until they heard someone's voice. It was a very familiar, plain voice. This particular voice was busy talking on a cell phone.

"Yes," said Mr. Protium. "I have six kids with various illnesses and two of which, have fallen from a high bra-" He turned, mid-sentence, to find Laura and Chris, with blood shot eyes, moaning in pain.

Mr. Protium rolled his eyes and said into his cell phone, "Make that eight kids."

*****

Sarita and Staci had been the only ones that weren't directly affected by Mr. Protium's grilling mishap. It's not like they weren't around, because they were. The two were only about a hundred feet away from Mr. Protium when he lit the match. Sarita and Staci were in the line of sight for each of the accidents, but they missed every single one. The girls were far too preoccupied.

Sarita and Staci were sitting on the grass, a short distance behind Mr. Protium, when the smoke rose. But the two missed it. Staci was busy trying to perfect a card trick while sarita was tending to a drooping flower. Neither one looked up when the dark cloud blew away, nor when Mr. Protium darted off into the far corner of the park. Both were isolated from the world, until a second gust of wind swept by, snatching a few of staci's cards.

"Hey!" she called in protest.

Staci shot to her feet and chased after her fleeing cards. Sarita looked up to see what was going on. She watched Staci run after her cards that fluttered in the breeze. Sarita quickly surveyed the park. *A lot had changed since I last looked*, she thought. Derrick and Xavier were having a conversation by the sidewalk. Curt, Hannah, Danny, and Jayden were lying on a hill sleeping, she assumed, with Mr. Protium a few feet away, on a prehistoric cell phone. Laura and Chris stumbled around blindly. Sarita thought they were playing some odd game. How could she have known any better? She turned her gaze to the grills. On the bench nearest to the food, she noticed Jared and me vomiting.

"Hmm," she said to herself. "When did that happen?"

Staci had returned with her cards when Sarita asked, "Do you think they're ok?" pointing to us gagging into the grass. Staci turned to us, cringed, then shrugged.

"Dunno. Wanna go check?" she asked. Sarita nodded and they headed in our direction.

Both, being on the varsity track team, Staci and Sarita were very swift and quite competitive: especially with each other. The two would constantly push each other to the limit and beyond; this would be no exception. Faster and faster, they ran, eyes locked, towards the target.

Maybe if one of the girls was looking in front of them instead of watching the other, they would've spotted the strategically placed branch hidden in the high grass. It was twice as unfortunate that they were both wearing shorts because, when Staci and Sarita reached the branch, they didn't just stumble, they were launched into the air. The two flew for a few seconds then fell abruptly onto a large patch of freshly broken glass and meteor pieces. Just another wonderful perk of Lincoln Memorial Park: Garbage *everywhere*.

The meteor infected glass shards sliced into the girls like a hot knife would slice into butter. They were hurt pretty badly. Their blood, refusing to clot, flowed freely. Through this entire ordeal, neither Staci nor Sarita shed a tear. They did wince, however, when their bones began to expand and contract as they, too, experienced the shock.

The two young women weren't all too concerned about their injuries. What mattered most was who had gotten the closest to the destination. Staci and Sarita struggled to their sides to analyze the situation. Shards of glass protruded from their appendages, but more importantly, they had tied. Pleased with the results, the girls let out a sigh of exhaustion and fainted.

Help arrived soon thanks to Kim Johnson who had called 911 a little while earlier, over-exaggerating her ailments. She told the police she was bleeding internally because she didn't think they'd come if she said she had a headache. The E.M.T.s rushed to the aid of the bleeding girls first and made their way to the rest of us. The school buses had arrived early at the request of Mr. Protium. The bus doors opened and the unaffected children loaded on as if nothing was wrong. Mr. Protium walked to the first of the two buses and boarded it. He leaned in and explained the situation to the nonchalant bus driver, got a head count of how many students were here, and exited. He did the same for the second bus. When he got off the second bus, Mr. Protium passed Xavier and Derrick, who were heading to the second bus. Xavier had a look in his eyes that made Mr. Protium pause. X looked worried and appeared to have something to say, but as X formed the right words; Derrick pulled him forcefully onto the bus. The doors closed behind the two and departed.

Mr. Protium, positive that the situation was now under control, ran to the ambulance and squeezed into the back with his injured students. The driver of the ambulance shut the back door. *We shoulda brought two cars*, he thought, and then hopped back into the driver's seat. As the packed ambulance pulled away, Mr. Protium wrinkled his nose at all the sickness that surrounded him and regretted not taking the day off…

*****

Derrick and Xavier were the only ones who knew exactly what was happening the entire day; in fact, they played a key role in all of it. When these two left our group, they went straight to work. So, while Mr. Protium was doing his best to prepare the grill, Derrick and Xavier were doing their best to prepare the park. They were the ones who broke the glass that Staci and Sarita fell on, hid the branch they tripped on, and made sure there were plenty of meteor pieces to go around. Derrick was the reason all the other students were acting so calm when the buses came. He convinced them all that nothing interesting was going to happen and when the time came to leave, they would pile into the buses without saying a word. While he spoke, Derrick's voice changed. It was oddly distorted; foreign. The voice he normally had was layered by what seemed like a second voice; one that had an alluring effect. They all obeyed Derrick's every word…as if under some spell or trace.

With their work finished, Derrick retired to the sidewalk and began to talk to each other.

"Everything is going as planned." Said Derrick as Staci and Sarita flew through the air. He smiled menacingly when they landed on the glass.

Xavier, on the other hand, looked nervous and somewhat stressed. He was worried for the safety of his friends, but his thoughts were interrupted by the arrival of the ambulance and school buses. The two teens were walking towards the second bus when they saw Mr. Protium. Derrick smiled innocently at the teacher, while Xavier looked at Mr. Protium solemnly. X considered asking how everyone was, but as he started to ask, Derrick pulled him away and onto the bus.

Taking at seat at the rear of the bus, Derrick and X watched as everyone was crowded into an ambulance that was obviously too small for that many people. Derrick cackled madly at the sight and, as he did so, his eyes transformed. They were now dark purple and his pupils were bright yellow.

"Well, the board is all set," Derrick said to Xavier in a strange, almost alien voice. "Are you ready to play, little brother?"

*****

It was 1:16 p.m. when we arrived at Mending Oaks Hospital. All 11 of us were carted through the E.R., past our friends Timmy, Brody, and Carrie who had some freaky skin rash. After everyone's condition stabilized, we were left in the Intensive Care Unit for observation. Visitors came and went, but everyone was too far-gone to notice anything; comatose and peaceful. This is the way we would stay until late that night when someone woke up.

At 11:55 p.m., Kim's heart rate spiked dangerously high. Nurses and doctors scurried to her room to find the source of the problem. By the time she was reached, Kim's heart reversed and was now dangerously low. Then, without notice, she flat-lined. A nearby nurse panicked and reached for a defibrillator. He charged it up and, after yelling "clear", pressed the pads firmly on Kim's chest. The voltage caused her body to jerk, but her heart still wasn't beating. The nurse tried again and again, to no avail; Still no pulse. A doctor walked over to the frantic nurse and touched his shoulder gently. When she spoke, time seemed to stand still.

"John," the doctor said slowly, "She's gone. You have to call it."

The nurse sighed and put down the instrument. He pulled back his sleeve, to reveal a wristwatch. "Time of Death: 11:59 P.M." With this, John the nurse covered Kim's face with a blanket and everyone left her room. The female doctor went to go call Kim's family and break the news while John stayed behind for a few moments.

"She was so young…" He whispered as he walked out of the room, closing the door behind him.

I said it once before and I'll say it again; Xavier Gonzalez was *never* wrong.

Chapter 5

"Incubation"

Incubation: To hatch by the warmth of the body.

It had been five months since the day our class went to Lincoln Park and everyday since then, our bodies had been hosts to foreign D.N.A. from the meteor; incubators to the unknown. For nearly half a year, we carried a new life form inside us, undisturbed. But on the fifth month, something hatched.

Kim had died and no one came to her funeral. Not because we were heartless jerks, but because no one was aware she was dead. Kim's mother was the only one who knew and since Kim had no real friends, nobody called to check on her. They all just assumed she had moved. My friends and I would've gone, but there was a slight problem: we were all in a comatose state. Everyone would remain this way, until we woke up five months later. After that time, we would return to the land of the living; but it wouldn't be that simple. The day had started out normal enough, but swiftly turned for the worst.

Brody Roselan had come to visit me that day (as he did everyday since the accident.) We had been best friends since we were in diapers. If I wasn't hanging out with Derrick, chances were high that I was with Brody. He stood at about 6 feet tall and was the type of guy that made you smile just by being around him. Brody was a very lanky kid with amber eyes who had often been described as a beanpole. He had a vanilla like skin tone and silver braces with blue rubber bands on them. Brody was infamous for his quick tongue. He had a comeback for everything and had an amazing poker face; it was difficult to tell

tell when he was lying. His mouth got him in trouble all too often, though.

Brody had something very important to tell me this time. He discovered something recently that would change his life forever. A few days prior to his visit, odd things began to happen to him. Odd *and* wonderful things if you asked him. The first bizarre occurrence was when Brody was in his room, playing video games. He was on the verge of beating his old high score, when his mom walked in.

"Brody, I *thought* I asked you to mow the lawn!" she roared.

"Yeah, I think you did too," he replied without pausing the game. "But I just didn't see the point."

"Oh?" she inquired. "And why is that?" This time, Brody stopped playing.

"Cuz," he said slyly, "We don't have a lawn."

Smarting off is what Brody did best and this occasion would be no different. Brody's mother found this funny (because it was just so ridiculous).

"Hm, that's interesting," she began as she walked to Brody's Curtain while he resumed his game. "Then what exactly do you call this?!"

Mrs. Roselan parted the curtains to reveal…nothing; nothing but dirt and the walkway that connects the house to the sidewalk.

"What the F…rench Toast?" she pondered aloud; refraining from cursing. "Where's the lawn?"

Brody joined his mom by the window and saw or didn't see what was once there. There truly was no lawn, just like he said…

Being the rational man that he was, Brody would've normally brushed off the incident as lawn thief if something similar hadn't happened the next day, at school. Brody hadn't done his homework and when his teacher asked for it, he gave the lamest excuse known to man: my dog ate it. His teacher wasn't buying it…until Brody's dog, Hoyt, strolled into the classroom

classroom randomly, coughed up the assignment, barked happily and then walked out. *How did this happen?* Brody wondered, but the answer was far too obvious.

While my science class went to Lincoln Park, Brody and his friends Carrie and Timmy decided to skip school. At first, the three couldn't agree on where to go, but when Timmy commented on how hot and humid it was, they knew what to do in an instant.

"The community pool will be empty on a school day," Brody reasoned and his friends agreed. So, with the plan to swim and relax, the three teens set out for the pool.

The Amy Caster memorial pool was empty, as Brody had concluded. Parking his truck near the entrance, the three exited and walked to the gate. Dark green bars, that interlocked to form a cage, surrounded the pool. Inside, several beach chairs were placed, evenly, around the area. The walkway was made of gray cement with tiny pebbles embedded in it. There wasn't a cloud in the sky that day.

"The perfect weather for swimming!" Timmy screamed as he cannonballed into the pool.

Carrie and Brody followed and in no time at all, the three had made quite a mess of the pool area.

While Brody and Timmy dunked each other underwater, Carrie decided to distance herself.

"You guys are a little too childish for my taste." She declared, although she was a year younger than the boys.

Gliding gracefully through the pool, Carrie swam her way to the deep end. She looked back at Timmy and Brody to see the two had moved their horseplay below the surface...to play rock, paper, scissors. She shook her head disapprovingly and wondered why boys that simple minded were allowed to roam freely. Carrie yawned slightly then propped her arms up on the outer rim of the pool and swam in place.

High above the three, two meteorites were falling fast. The smaller rock changed directions; then began to chase a bus and entered through an open window; while the other, baseball sized fragment had its own destination: the community pool.

Carrie's eyes were shut as she soaked in all the sunlight. Brody had Timmy forcefully submerged and Timmy flailed around in protest; inadvertently drinking half the pool in the process. The meteorite landed silently, slicing through the surface of the water as smoothly as a hot knife through butter. Timmy stopped struggling when he saw it sinking to the bottom.

What's that? He thought. The rock descended deeper and deeper until it was sucked into the pool's filter. In less than a second, it hit the fan and was blended into a fine powder then combined with the pool water to form repulsive meteor goo. After, the slimy space substance was then unleashed into the pool once more.

The goo, as if magnetized, began to stick to the three teens at an alarming rate; covering their entire bodies like an extra layer of skin.

"Get it off!" Carrie yelped when she noticed it.
She jumped out of the pool, shaking frantically, trying to free herself from the unwelcome exoskeleton. Brody and Timmy, however, were a bit less freaked out.

"Dude!" said Timmy as he scrapped some off his chest and smelled it.

It smelled rancid. Timmy gagged and hopped out of the pool, running for the pool showers. Brody wasn't far behind and in no time at all the friends were hosing off the goo. But they now had a dilemma: when the slime was gone; a horrifying skin rash was left. Carrie, Brody, and Timmy were covered head to toe in disgusting, abrasive lumps and felt the shock that was all too familiar to everyone after being infected.

Frightened by their green exterior, the teens piled into Brody's truck and sped to Mending Oaks Hospital. By 1:14 p.m., they were sitting in the hospital's waiting room; filling out paperwork. Two minutes later, my injured friends and I were wheeled through the waiting room, past Brody and his friends, on our way to the E.R. The Doctor saw the three shortly after and prescribed a treatment that would come to cure the odd skin mutation a few days later.

Brody was hell-bent on telling me about everything that I had missed, including his strange ability, but when he arrived at my room, something happened that made Brody forget why he even came. He was fortunate enough to have front row seats to the show.

The Emily Burley wing of Mending Oaks was isolated and quiet. You had to walk around to the back of Mending Oaks and travel down a walkway for about 3 minutes before you arrived at the destination. Through the two swinging brown doors, there were 10 rooms; 5 on each side of the ill-lit hallway. On the left side of the hall the rooms of Jayden, Chris, Mine, Curt, Sarita could be found. While on the right, there was Jared, Laura, Danny, Hannah and Staci.

It was at 1:16 p.m., a full five months after our accidents, that the Burley wing of Mending Oaks erupted with life and it began with me. Brody peered into each room until he found mine (he did this every visit; just in case they moved me. They never did.) But what he saw made his heart skip a beat.

According to Brody, when he entered the room, I was engulfed in a large ball of fire and levitating over my bed; unconscious. The immense heat of the flames had incinerated the heart monitoring equipment. Brody hurried to my aid but was repelled out the door by a miniature explosion from the center of the fire. He tried to scream for help, but his lips defied him.

Brody propped himself up in the hallway and checked for injuries. He winced when he felt that he had about 4 or 5 broken ribs from the impact; two of which pierced through his skin and were quite visible. Blood trickled from the open wounds but Brody was strangely calm.

"Dude," he said, "This is my favorite shirt." He sighed then said, "Uh, my ribs are healed and back in place. Oh, and my wounds are closed and not infected at all." Like magic, his blood reversed its outward flow and the ribs were back to normal.

This is so cool! Brody thought. Suddenly, he realized his pants were moist. It couldn't be blood, he reasoned. "Oh, Dear God, please don't let me have wet myself..." He whispered.

To Brody's relief, it wasn't urine; it was water and a lot of it. It was everywhere.

"What the F..." He lost his words when he saw the source of the liquid. Two doors down, on the other side of the hall, Jared's room was being flooding and it wasn't coming from rain or a broken water valve, but from...Jared.

Water was bursting from under the door. Inside, encased in solid ice, was Jared; still in a coma. The ice cube had cracks in its sides from which the water gushed. The breaks grew larger by the seconds as more fluids squeezed through. Moments later, the cube abruptly shattered; unleashing a frightening surge of water into the room. Filling the place to the ceiling in a matter of seconds, the tidal wave cut through Jared's door like scissors through flimsy paper and spread through the halls.

When Brody saw the approaching onslaught, he hopped to his feet to run but it was too late. The wave swept by my room, extinguished the flames and began to carry Brody to the end of the hall until an unseen force started to pull him back.

A miniature tornado had formed one door down from Jared; with Laura at the eye of the storm. When the floodwaters combined with the cyclone, a deadly whirlpool emerged. It swiftly blossomed into a monstrous water vacuum that stiff chairs and ugly plastic plants gravitated towards. Brody was trapped underwater by the swirling hole of doom. *This...sucks. A lot.* He thought. He tried to swim free but his efforts were futile. The windows in Laura's room cracked under the pressure and water poured out of them, though it wasn't enough to aid the situation. It had crossed Brody's mind to *Will* away the water with his ability but decided against it.

I'll drown for sure if I try to talk, he thought.

Not that it mattered much. He had about 20 more seconds to live anyway.

Incubation

The entire hall was drenched in 6 feet of water and Jared's, Laura's and my room were equally soaked. As Brody began to give up resisting, the ground started quaking. But this was no average earthquake; more like a 7.0 on the Richter scale and Chris was the epicenter.

Across the hall, in Chris's room, ghastly fissures opened and traveled down the hall in every direction, swallowing miscellaneous objects that were unfortunate enough to be in the way. From various sections of the cracks, stone pillars sprouted; puncturing holes in the ceiling. Back in the room, where Chris's bed should have been, there was a solid granite platform and on this platform was a coffin-like structure made of light brown sandstone. Inside, Chris laid motionless; sleeping like a baby.

The newly formed fissures acted as giant drains and in moments, there were only trace amounts of water present in the wing. This pleased Brody who, after coughing up about a gallon of water, began to kiss the mildly soggy teal carpet. But his relief was short lived when he heard a foreboding snap from above, followed by an elongated cracking sound.

Laura's cyclone had just subsided when the ceiling began to sink inward. The Emily Burley wing of Mending Oaks was collapsing with everyone inside it. Brody rushed to try and get his friends out in time; aided by the newly awakened Jared, Laura and me. Chris's stone casing splintered into millions of jagged fragments and rocketed in all directions; We avoided the larger pieces but many of the smaller ones lightly grazed the four of us. The platform Chris was lying on crumbling beneath him and he hit the ground with a sharp thud that jolted him awake. We filled him in on the situation and he was eager to help.

The five of us split up to cover more ground. Jared went to get Hannah, Laura headed to Curt's room, Chris looked for Danny, Brody had Staci and I planned to save Jayden.

*****

When Jared arrived at Hannah's room, there was a problem: it was empty. Or, at least, it appeared to be. Taking a closer look, he noticed that the sheets on the bed were raised and outlined a body that resembled Hannah's. The floor began to buckle under his feet, so, deciding not to question it, Jared grabbed the invisible girl and darted for the exit.

*****

Oh, God. Oh, God, Laura thought as she rushed to Curtis's room. *Please don't be dead, Curt. We gotta get outta here.* She was sure that her Aunt Karen would have her head if Curt died. She shook Curt violently to wake him.

"Wake up, cousin. Please. We have to go. *now!*" She screeched. *Hannah needs you, Curt. You have to get up...* she thought.

"Where's...Hannah? Is she alright?" Curt said as he regained consciousness. Laura was elated. Her cousin wasn't dead.

"She'll be fine. We all will be." Laura assured him, getting her timid composure back. "But we have to go. Like now."

Laura helped Curt out of bed and as the two walked away, she couldn't help but wonder how Curt heard what was never said. It was almost as if he read her mind...

*****

Danny was wide-awake when Chris showed up.

"Hey dude," said Danny calmly. "What's up?"

Chris didn't reply. He was speechless, in fact; and with good reason. Danny...was a dog. Literally. A Border Collie, to be specific.

"Um, dude." Chris squeaked out at last. "You're a dog." Danny yipped with glee in response.

"I know! This is light years beyond awesome. Look what I can do!" He stated as he demonstrated his new tricks. Danny scratched the back of his ear with his paw, chased his tail for a while and began to lick his crotch. Chris turned in disgust.

"Ah! Stop, dude. Stop. That's so gross, man." Danny sat back down on his hind legs.

"You're just jealous, kid. That's ok. I'll let you hate on me." Chris was prepared to comment on how White he just sounded when the earth quaked again; interrupting him. Snapping back into reality, Chris declared that they had to get out or they'd die. Danny barked in agreement and they left.

*****

Brody had no idea where he was. He walked into Staci's room, but something was wrong. He could've sworn that he was still in the hospital, but nothing was destroyed or burned or broken.

"I know where I am..." Brody whispered to himself. "This is my room. How'd I get here?"

It was indeed Brody's room. Standing in the center of his room, he saw his flat screen T.V. and video games. To his right was his ceiling high window that overlooked his lawnless front yard. Behind him was his door, covered in movie posters and pictures of attractive female celebrities. And to his left, was Staci, propped up in Brody's bed, reading. Shoes still on, she was engrossed in a romance novel she found under Brody's mattress.

"You've got an interesting taste in literature, Brody." Staci laughed. He was dumb struck.

"What are you doing here? You're supposed to be at the hospital. I'm supposed to be at the hospital. How'd we get here?!" Brody was frantic.

Staci earmarked her page and said, "Hey, be cool. It's an illusion. We're still at the hospital. I don't know how, but I think I'm doing this." Her statement confused Brody even more.

"What do you mean 'You're doing this'? You gotta undo this so we can leave!"

"I.D.K. how!" She retorted.

"What?" Brody asked.

"I said I don't know how. Jeeze, brush up on you're I.M. speak." Staci was enjoying this way too much and Brody had had enough.

"This illusion isn't real! We're at the hospital again!" demanded Brody forcefully and, as expected, Brody's room melted away with the help of his power; revealing that they were, indeed, still in the hospital.

"W.T.F., mate? How'd you do that?" Staci protested.

"What does that even mean?!" asked the frustrated Brody. Staci smirked and rose from her hospital bed.

"Oh, would you look at the time. We gotta go. I'll explain later. I promise."

Brody sent her a chilling glare.

"F.Y.I., I hate you." He said.

Staci smiled again. "Hey, you're learning."

*****

My mission was going surprisingly well. Jayden seemed to be normal. No weird occurrences; well, at least not yet. But I'm getting ahead of myself. I found Jayden's room easily enough, woke her up and almost made it out, but the ceiling had other plans.

The entire left side of the Burley Wing collapsed without notice; burying the two of us in debris. Surely, we would have been killed…if it weren't for our numerous, leafy saviors.

Enormous Oak Trees bloomed and rescued us from a shallow grave; I suppose we owe Sarita a "Thank You" card. The roots of the trees all originated in her room. One look inside revealed Sarita in a make shift cage of dense vines and what appeared to be bamboo. With a weak Jayden at my side, we scaled the mountain of rubble that was once a part of the hospital. Sarita's cage had disbanded when we arrived and she was a bit disoriented but we really didn't have time to waste; we grabbed her from her bed and ran for the front door like we stole something.

*****

The Emily Burley wing completely caved in immediately after everyone was safely out. South of the former wing, was the community garden. It was populated by a rainbow of flowers and, towards its center, there was a grass plot with 5 or 6 stone benches. We regrouped there. Hannah was visible once again and Danny was no longer a canine. We waited until our hearts stopped beating at 100 miles an hour before we tried to talk. And even when we could speak, not much came out. Eyes wide, breathing heavily, we just kinda stared at each other, wondering if any of this was real.

The main part of Mending Oaks was completely undisturbed. Doctors, back from their lunch breaks, entered the automatic doors without a glance in our direction. ER patients came and went. A Caucasian family, bearing "Get Well Soon" balloons, went through the doors as well. We were all very curious as to why no one noticed the newly demolished wing of the hospital, but we said nothing. Actually, no one said much of anything for the longest time until Danny decided to break the silence.

"Um, guys..." he whispered, "What are we?" It was a simple question and yet none could answer it.

*****

Derrick and Xavier were the culprits responsible for everyone's obliviousness. Hours before Brody's visit, Derrick paid a visit of his own; to the receptionist's desk. Using the loud speaker, he easily mesmerized any and everyone in the immediate area. So, to them, the Emily Burley wing of Mending Oaks was untouched and empty; they didn't hear or see anything out of the ordinary.

Now perched on a ledge of Mending Oaks, feet dangling freely over the edge, Derrick and X watched us closely.

"You sure you don't wanna drop out now, Drahc'ir?" Derrick said to X.

"Don't call me that, Sivart! My name is Xavier now."

Derrick rolled his eyes. "Whatever, Bro. Give up now. The birthright is naturally mine. I am the first-born. I don't even know why we have this retarded contest."

Xavier smiled at this. "It's not over, til it's over, *bro*. You're sounding a little nervous." X was under Derrick's skin and he knew it. Derrick didn't like this and was going to respond...when his pocket started to vibrate. It was his phone; he had a text message. It read:

Get home now. It's time for phase two. – Dad.

"Ugh. Time to Go." Said Derrick and he rose to his feet.

"I'll race you." Xavier offered.

"You don't stand a chance." Derrick countered.

"We'll see." Said a confident Xavier.

They were both on their feet now and, on a count of three, the two rocketed straight up into space; leaving no evidence of their presence aside from the ear-shattering boom left when they broke the sound barrier.

Chapter 6

"Manipulation"

Manipulation: To adapt or change to suit one's purpose or advantage.

A few days had passed since the incubation. We pieced together the story of what happened with the aid of Brody and, as he explained, we came to the realization that we had been changed; mutated. We had special abilities but we couldn't control them, at least, not yet.

It was summer now, school was out and, besides catching up on five months of make up work and physical therapy, our schedule was empty. Brody suggested that we practice, figure out how our powers worked. Everyone knew what they could do, we were just alittle foggy on the extent of things. And, while we tried to get our acts together, something else was going down, light years away, which would prove to be bigger than all of us.

Derrick and Xavier flew for hours through the empty vacuum of space until arriving upon an oval planet decorated with hues of coral. The two descended slowly, and then skidded to a stop. The smell of burnt rubber permeated from their tennis shoes.

A quick survey showed the surface was desolate; no structures, landforms or sinkholes. A soft breeze carried a cloud of dust and sand, aimlessly, in the distance. Derrick roamed around until he stumbled upon a cell phone shaped stone.

"Here we go." He said when he saw it.

Xavier stood by his brother and, in unison they exclaimed: "Flesruoy laever, Nagem ot etag!"

Their command caused the cell phone stone to vibrate like it was ringing. The shaking grew to a greater intensity and the ground around the stone began to part and an elevator materialized from within. The doors opened with a "ding" and the two boarded it. The doors glided to a close again and the elevator retreated below the surface.

The inside of the elevator was lined with navy blue carpet with pale orange spots and squiggly lines, randomly, through out. Stale elevator muzak filled the room. Above the door, there was a panel that told you what floor you were on. To the left of the door, the wall was covered, from ceiling to floor, in buttons; each going to a different level. Listed in numerical order, there were 473 floors in all; 475 if you counted the buttons that take you to the surface and to the basement. Xavier pressed the basement button and it illuminated on contact.

The elevator darted downward at a startling speed, and the panel above the door "binged" as it passed each floor. Derrick and Xavier stood, awkwardly silent, as this all occurred. Minutes passed and the elevator came to a halt. The doors opened with a "ding" and the siblings exited.

They entered a dim, narrow corridor riddled with the stench of motor oil and daisies. The floor was laced with some type of minor adhesive that stuck to the bottom of Derrick and Xavier's melted shoes. There were magenta, wooden doors on the left and right side of the hall; each labeled in some odd, alien language. At the end of the hall, a blinding white light could be seen.

The two teens walked into the light and, once their eyes adjusted themselves, they scanned the room for their target. Derrick and Xavier had entered a dome shaped room. Various foreign machines covered the walls to the ceiling. Lights, on the machines, flashed periodically throughout the room; in various colors.

The floor appeared to be made of bleach white marble; heavily scuffed from repeated pacing. All along the walls, there were odd creatures that looked like many different animals spliced together; each was monitoring a machine. Some even had hover packs to reach the higher ones. All the animals turned to look when Derrick and Xavier entered the room. Each mutant creature reached for his or her strangely colored and shaped pistols (which were quadruple barreled and the trigger was located on the top of the gun) that were placed in each of their holsters.

The two boys stopped when they saw the hostile creatures and, with his right hand, Derrick reached up and pressed something behind his right earlobe; X did the same. The image of the teens flickered like a T.V. with a poor signal when they did this and, not long after, Derrick and Xavier didn't look human at all, but then again, they weren't. It was a well-kept secret that no one else knew; Derrick and Xavier were aliens.

Derrick's true form had the body of a bronze colored rhino with the wings of a silver bat and the legs of a light brown camel; he would be best described as a bizarre centaur. While X looked like a kangaroo with dragonfly wings and the feet of an elephant.

The once hostile aliens dropped down to their knees; bowing and chanting: "All hail Prince Drahc'ir and Prince Sivart!"

In the center of the room, there were two escalators that led to and from a large platform; floating in midair. The worker animals rolled out pink carpet from Derrick and Xavier (or Sivart and Drahc'ir, as the creatures called them) to the escalator.

"Man, I missed the royal treatment. 16 earth years is way too long of a time to be away from home." Derrick stated in his native tongue, which sounded similar to backwards German. X was silent; he did not want to be back.

On the platform, their were two rose colored thrones with two creatures occupying them. The larger throne held a masculine, purple gorilla with the head, neck and tail of a coral snake.

In the other, smaller, throne, there was a feminine Bengal Tiger with the wings of an eagle. They both had dark violet eyes with canary yellow pupils; as did Xavier and Derrick.

To the right of the thrones, there was a bulletin board covered with pictures of humans; my friends and I were on there. They were random snapshots; taken by a voyeur (100 pictures total). Each photo was like a trading card because, on the backs of all the pictures, there were statistics on that person; Birthday, Age, Height, Weight, Power, Residence, etc.

Xavier ran to the tiger-eagle hybrid. "Mommy! I missed you so much! Earth years move by ever so slowly." He said in Seoreh, their native language.

The two greeted each other in warm embrace.

"I missed you as well, my little Drahc'ir. How have you been, my child?" Xavier's mother enquired, still in Seoreh. And while the mother and son exchanged pleasantries, Derrick was all business.

Derrick bowed to the gorilla-snake hybrid. "Father, I am ready. Everything went according to plan on Earth. The meteors you sent were quite effective. I am prepared for phase two."

Xavier released his mother and stood next to his brother. "I, too, am ready, father. Probably more ready than Sivart could ever be." X added.

Derrick scoffed at this. "You're *face* is probably more ready that I could ever be." He spit back.

"That made no sense." Xavier defended.

"You're *face* made no sense." Derrick countered.

"Enough!" Their father interjected. "You are both well prepared for the Tsol Battle Championship. Now, remember you're fighting for the honor of our dear planet, Chorifer, the title of Tsol Battle Champion and the three rule free wishes that accompany the title. This TBC's competition is stiff. You're playing against the best in the universe, and they're hungry to win; you two must be equally as hungry."

The King paused and reached under his throne; he pulled out a dark green, heavily aged chest. The King of Chorifer unhooked the double latches that held the box shut and raised the lid to unveil large gemstones of various shapes and hues; each stone connected to indestructible titanium chains. There were 20 stones inside the case; each bearing a golden "C", for Chorifer, centered on the front.

The King lifted a Sapphire Star and placed it around Derrick's neck. He, then, picked up a Ruby Heart and gave it to Xavier.

"My sons," The Queen resumed where the King had left off. "I know this is your first time entering the TBC, so, just know there are no rules to the game *except*: don't lose your medallions. If you lose your medallions, you are out of the competition. As princes of Chorifer, you shall have first pickings of the humans. Choose five and only five for your team. Take care of your team and they shall take care of you."

"To reach the semi-finals in the Tsol Battle Championship," The King tagged in. "You each will need five medallions. You can steal your competitors' medallions or fight for them but you are not restricted to just these two options; be creative. Also, if any of your pawns die, you are eliminated and your medallions will teleport to your nearest adversary. Any questions?" Derrick and Xavier shook their heads. "Very well then. Choose your humans wisely and return to earth to assemble your teams. Do not forget: All of the 18 remaining competitors are somewhere but it's up to you to locate them."

Derrick and X moved to the bulletin board of pictures and examined the fronts and backs of each one; trying to form a team that was not only balanced but powerful. Derrick selected Jared, Laura, Curt, Staci, and Jayden; while Xavier went with Me, Chris, Hannah, Danny and Sarita.

"Interesting," The Queen observed. "Of all the humans, you chose the one's you are most familiar with."

"And what's even more interesting," The King commented. "Is that you two have 'Best Friends', I believe they're called, fighting on opposing sides; as well as 'Boyfriends versus

Girlfriends'. This may prove to be entertaining." The alien brothers nodded in agreement.

"Sivart, my son, please do not be angry. I realize that it is the birth right of every Chorifian first born son to compete in the TBC, but since your brother was born 3 seconds after you, he, too, has the right to compete. I have the utmost faith that the stronger of you will be victorious."

"Don't worry, father. I will be." Derrick and Xavier replied, in unison and then frowned at each other.

"One more thing, my children," The Queen added as the two had turned to leave. She reached under her throne this time and pulled out two medium sized jewelry boxes. A steady beeping resonated from the cases. The Queen opened the boxes to reveal radars that looked like average digital watches. The wristbands were a few sizes too large but when Derrick and X put them on their left wrists, the bands shrunk to fit. The face of the radar was green with a diameter length yellow line that moved clockwise and beeped every time it completed a full rotation.

"These radars will aid in your search for the five medallions you will need for the semi-finals. The golden 'C' on each of the medallions is a tracking device that cannot be removed. The radar detects any and every medallion within 100 miles of you and, if there are none that close, it points you in the direction of the nearest one. That is all. Be safe and watch your backs."

Xavier hugged his mom and Derrick bowed to his dad again then they stepped on the down escalator, walked down the pink carpet once more, past the formally hostile worker hybrids, down the dark corridor and entered the elevator. Xavier pressed the "surface" button on the control panel, then the doors slid shut and the elevator shot upward.

The lightning fast ride ended as quickly as it began and the two brothers had reached the surface of Chorifer. The ground opened and the elevator poked out. The teens, having changed back to their human forms on the way up, exited swiftly and the elevator vanished below the surface.

"Ugh. I hate this body. What good are fingers? And why don't humans have four legs? It would make life so much easier." Derrick complained. *Oh, shut up. Seriously.* Xavier thought.

Suddenly, the radar watches began to ring like telephones. A startled Derrick jumped but X just looked at the watch. The face was no longer a radar; it was like a computer monitor. "Call From: Mom" flashed in yellow and "Answer Call" blinked in red below it. Derrick and Xavier pressed "Answer Call" and the watches projected a hologram of their mother.

"I believed it would be easier to demonstrate this feature rather then explain it. The radar is also a communicator. It will work anywhere in the galaxy. It's voice activated; just say 'Call' and state the name of whom you wish to call. Also, before I go, there is one serious matter I had neglected to tell you earlier. I know you know that if you lose all your medallions or if any of your humans die, you are eliminated from the competition. But what your father and I did not tell you is that, if you lose, you will be teleported to a holding cell in an undisclosed location where you will stay until the Death Bringer comes and relieves you of your soul as well as the souls of your humans." The Queen paused for a moment to let the information sink in then continued. "You know how to reach your father and I. Goodbye, my sons. And I hope to see at least one of you again."

The call ended and the Queen's image faded. This new knowledge was a blow to the gut. Only one of them would come back alive; if they were lucky. So, with heavy hearts and clouded minds, Derrick and Xavier flew back to earth in dead silence.

*****

Back on earth, my friends and I were at Lincoln Park, trying to get our abilities to work; it wasn't going so well. We were almost at a breaking point when, out of the sky, Derrick and Xavier landed in front of us. Their clothes were burned and full of holes from when they re-entered the atmosphere. Everyone was speechless. Those of us that were standing fell to the ground in shock.

"Hey, guys..." Xavier said after a moment. "We have...uh...some explaining to do."

We were blown away. Derrick and X explained everything. About them being aliens, (they showed us, actually. That was a weird experience. Chris may or may not have wet himself alittle) and about the contest thingy. The two even told us that their home planet had sent the meteors that infected us. It was too much to grasp at one time. Derrick and X said that they knew how to make our powers work but we were too freaked out to understand. So, we decided to meet again the next day for training purposes and whatnot. They told us they'd call with details of when and where to meet but only when the time was right.

The next day came and nothing happened. Hours passed and the phone never rang. It wasn't til about 7:00 p.m. that anyone heard anything from our alien friends. Derrick sent a text message to Jared, Laura, Curt, Jayden and Staci to meet at his house.

The five arrived at Derrick's plain, white wash, two-story house. The lawn was perfectly green, despite the season, and neatly trimmed. Derrick's mailbox was black with white letters that read "McGuire" and stood erect. I had never noticed before but Derrick's house was perfect; and not in the good way. It was as if no one lived there. Compared to the other houses, Derrick's stood out.

The five teens were at the front door by 7:17 p.m., about to knock, when Derrick called to them from the backyard.

"Guys!" He yelled. "I'm out back. Go through the side gate."

To the left of the house was the side gate. Jared and company found it and went through.

Derrick's backyard was just as plain and ordinary as his front yard, with the exception of the massive Oak tree in the dead center of the yard. The sun was blindingly bright so the teens to refuge under the tree's shadow.

"I'm so glad you could make it." Hissed Derrick menacingly. "We're got a lot of work to do. First, you must harness you ability, then manipulate it to your advantage and, finally, defeat my little brother and his pathetic excuse of a team! Killing them, if the need arises."

Jared and his friends were in complete agreement with everything Derrick was saying…until he got to the whole "killing people" part.

"Whoa, dude. Whoa. We were all for you teaching us about our powers and stuff. We were also down with the contest or whatevs, but we draw the line at killing our friends over some stupid alien game. Thanks but no thanks. We're out. Later, Derrick." Protested Jared as he stood and led his friends back to the gate.

Derrick found this funny and laughed.

"How cute. But the thing is," he called to them in an odd, hypnotic voice that sounded like his normal voice fused with another, deeper, voice. "I don't remember giving you humans a choice in the matter. Come back here, *now*." The five hypnotized teens returned to their places on command and awaited further instruction. "Good. And *never* call me Derrick again. My name is Sivart. Prince Sivart. Don't you ever forget that."

"Yes, Prince Sivart." They replied in a monotone unison. Derrick smirked at this.

"Very good. Now…where were we?"

*****

Xavier called Chris, Hannah, Danny, Sarita and I at 7:18 p.m. to meet him back at Lincoln Park. The sun would set in two hours, but you couldn't tell by how sunny it was when we got there. We met on the benches by the grill that Jared and I had our eating contest near.

"Hey, X." I started when we gathered.

"You're friends are gone." He said flatly.

"What do you mean?" The others asked, still surprised that Xavier could talk.

"My brother has used his hypnotique, hypnotizing technique, on your friends and now they're under his spell. He's training them to kill as we speak. Sivart will attack soon so we must be prepared."

"Intuition?" I questioned.

"Intuition." He responded.

I sighed. "Guys, Xavier is never wrong, so, listen up. What do you need us to do?"

X thought about it.

"I need you all to show me your powers. But before you do that, I must tell you that each of your talents are directly linked to your life force. If you do too much, you will feel physically fatigued and whenever that happens, stop and rest. If you push yourself any further than that, you may die. However, the more you use your ability, the greater your resistance to death will be. For-" Hannah raised her hand as if she was in school and interrupted X.

"Yes, um, Heather."

"It's Hannah." She snapped, mildly annoyed. "How do we *show* you our powers? Cuz, like, I dunno how to do that."

"Good question. Your abilities are controlled by your emotions. I recommend being level headed when you use them. Your powers can be unpredictable and dangerous if you use them when upset or scared. Just relax and don't force it; let it flow."

Hannah tried it out first. She was really worried about Curt's safety but she knew panicking wouldn't help the situation so she cleared her mind. She remembered the day of mutation at Lincoln Park 5 months ago. She recalled the peacefulness of lying on that hill under the cloudless sky, holding hands with her boyfriend, then, like magic, Hannah disappeared. It started with her feet and ended at her head. Everyone was amazed. Hannah, who had been sitting on a tabletop, was now walking around, but all that anyone could see of her were the footprints that were formed in the grass with every step she took.

"O.M.G. I love this. But...how do I turn back?" Came Hannah's voice from seemingly nowhere.

"Oh, right. Just concentrate and it will happen." X said; and he was right.

Hannah focused on being visible and it happened all at once. She was a quick study; jumping back and forth between visibility and invisibility.

"I could get used to this. Thank you, King and Queen of Chorifer." Hannah giggled as she became visible again.

"Dude, me next. Me next." Exclaimed an excited Danny. "Obviously, I'm like a shape shifter. But what all can I change into?" He asked X.

"Excellent question as well. Since your power and Hannah's power changes your physical state, using your power for a prolonged period of time could get you stuck that way forever. As for your specific limitations, you can turn into any life form that you've ever seen; including things from television or literature."

"Word dog!" Danny yelled as he transformed into a bald eagle and, instinctively, soared into the air. His clothes were left in the grass as he did spirals in the sky. *Hm, that might be a problem when I change back.* He thought.

Danny dove down and snatched his clothes up with his talons then ascended to a nearby tree to change back and hide his nudity.

"Hey, Xavier. Quick question." He called from the tree as he dressed himself. "I know you said I could be any life form and all, so, I'm assuming, humans count in that. But what if I shape shifted into Hannah, would I be able to go invisible too?"

"No."

"Oh..." he whispered, disappointed.

"Not yet." X added to his previous statement.

"Oh!" Danny climbed down and rejoined his friends. "When will I be able to?"

"I'll let you know when you're ready."

"Word?"

"Um, yeah. Word."

"Now, Frankie, Chris, and Sarita, your powers are slightly different from Danny and Hannah's. You three have elemental abilities. Frankie creates and manipulates fires, Chris does the same with earth and minerals, as does Sarita; only with plants and organisms of that nature. So, controlling your abilities will be a bit different. Once you use them for the first time, you will have to suppress your powers until you are ready to use them or they will be on 24/7. Sarita, you try it. Clear your mind and flow."

Sarita was eager to start and she began well but soon lost control. Grass sprouted from every pore in her body and ravenous tree roots and vines burst from the soil and embraced her then carried her several yards in the air. More plants appeared and those grabbed the rest of us and lifted us up as well but apparently they didn't like us as much as Sarita, because the vines began to spin us around rapidly.

"Sarita! Stop! You're making me sick!" Chris screeched as he swayed back and forth swiftly. The vines surrounding us were squeezing tightly; constricting our breathing. Danny and Xavier were on the verge of passing out.

"Sarita," Xavier gasped. "Suppress your power. It's the only way."

Sarita concentrated hard and the vines retracted into the ground and released their chokehold on us. Sarita shed her grassy layer of skin and laughed.

"That was a rush. Is everyone ok?" We all nodded, shakily. "Ok. Good." She said with a smile.

"Well done, Sarita. Just remember to stay calm and collected or you will lose control like that again. Chris, it's your turn."

"Oh, jeez." Chris mumbled and closed his eyes. Moments later, stone spikes protruded from all over Chris's body. Chucks of earth were ripped from the ground, launched into the air and floated there. Chris opened his eyes. The patch of grass and dirt he was standing on rose 5 feet in mid air. His spikes sprang from his body in every direction but, since he was hovering above our heads, we were safe from harm. The floating dirt clumps were in orbit around Chris and new spikes replaced the ones from before. The rest of us watched silently; afraid of what would happen next. The ground began to quake beneath us and gave birth to miniature canyons. The table that Xavier and I were sitting on slid into one of the cracks; we hopped off just in time.

Focus and suppress. I am in control. Chris thought. The jagged caverns closed, crushing the table to pieces. The floating dirt clods fell to the ground, abruptly, and Chris fired all the remaining spikes into an open field; where they landed harmlessly. He, then, sauntered back down to Earth.

"Let's do that again!" Chris suggested.

"Um, how bout we don't and say we did?" I answered.

"Well, I'd like to see you do better." He fired back.

"Fine, I will."

"Ok, do it."

"I'm doing it."

"I don't see anything."

"Just gimme a second."

Here we go, I thought. I tried to clear my mind but it was impossible. I kept flashing back to how Sarita and Chris lost control. What if I did that? Uncontrolled fire? There were trees and dry brush everywhere. The whole place would go up in smoke. I was getting cold feet about this. I tried to use my powers but it wasn't working.

"I think we got the gist of our powers." I copped out.

"I agree. You all have done well. Go home and practice often. I'll call when I need you." Xavier concurred. I think he sensed my fear.

"Wait, we should have a name. Like a group name!" Danny explained. It was a good idea. We all brainstormed for a while and, several shot down suggestions later, Hannah had something. A few weeks before our comas, our history teacher, Mr. Drymore, taught us about a military formation used in ancient Europe that was very efficient in defending themselves against their enemies.

"What about…the Phalanx?"

It was perfect.

"I like it," said X. "Ok, Phalanx. Go home and pract-" Xavier was interrupted by his wristwatch/radar. It was blaring unexpectedly. He checked the screen. There was a bright yellow dot moving rapidly towards the center of the radar. Xavier's face flushed pale.

"What's up, X?" I asked.

"Someone is coming for my medallion. I didn't foresee an attack from my brother so soon but it's too late now. So, I must ask you all a very serious question: Are you ready for round one?"

Chapter 7

"Confrontation"

Confrontation: The clashing of forces or ideas.

The yellow dot was closing in and we searched in all directions for the oncoming threat. I thought my heart was gonna burst from chest. After what felt like centuries, a silver 4-door SUV with tinted windows pulled into the Lincoln Park parking lot.

An elderly Anglo Saxon woman stepped out of the driver's side door, pulling a wooden cane out with her. On the passenger side, an equally old, Moroccan man exited. From the backseat, a white newly wed couple, no older than 30, slid out the left side door and out the right, came a Caucasian punk teenager with an MP3 player in his shirt pocket, headphones blaring with heavy metal music. Behind him, a little Asian girl, about 4 or 5 years old, climbed out. She dragged a dirty, old stuffed rabbit (by the ear) along with her. They were all dressed in white jumpsuits and white tee shirts like some bad pop band, but one thing was certain; this wasn't Derrick.

The 6 met us by the benches. Around the elderly woman's neck, there was an Emerald Pentagon Shaped Medallion.

"Excuse me, sweetie," The woman croaked. "Is that there medallion yours?" She was talking to X.

"Yes. Yes, it is." He responded.

"Oh. Oh, dear. I'm afraid I'm going to have to fight you for it, honey. Unless, of course, you want to just hand it over."

X had a serious look on his face. It was clear he wasn't handing anything over, not without a fight.

"Very well, dear." She smiled, "Attack!" The elderly woman's calm demeanor was gone and her team of misfits sprang into action.

The time worn Moroccan man teleported with a blinding flash of light, reappeared behind Hannah moments later, latched on to her and was gone again.

The newly wed couple was holding hands when they approached Sarita.

"Aw, she's so adorable. Babe, lets go adopt a little girl after we kill this one." The woman expressed.

"We'll see." Replied her husband and, with their free hands, they hoisted Sarita hundreds of feet in the air (using telekinesis) and heaved her across the park.

"Oh. We got some distances on that one, honey." The wife said as they watched Sarita soaring through the sky.

The innocent little girl walked up to Chris alone; her rabbit was nowhere in sight.

"Do you wanna play with me?" she asked cheerfully.

Chris laughed. "Yeah, right, kid."

She frowned and someone tapped Chris's shoulder. He wheeled around to see the little girl's stuffed rabbit. Only, it wasn't stuffed anymore; it was huge, buff, and rabid looking. The deranged rabbit was foaming at the mouth.

"Wrong answer." It seethed and sucker punched Chris through a tree.

It was Danny who initiated the punk rocker teen.
"Oh, you're tough. What do you do? You gonna rock me to death? You don't scare me."

The punk teen had about 3 inches on Danny, height wise. He took out the ear bud in his right ear.

"What'd you say? I couldn't hear ya." Danny's face burned red with anger.

"Oh, a comedian." Danny shifted into a vicious Timber wolf. "Let's see how funny you are when I rip you to shreds."

"Aw, you make a cute puppy."

"Stop talking and bring it." The punk turned off his MP3 player and put it in his front pocket.

"Be careful what you wish for." He said to Danny and, with this, the punk teen multiplied into 200 copies of himself and surrounded Danny. "Did I bring it well enough for you? Cuz if not, I can always make more." The 200 teens said in eerie unison.

Danny's tail shot between his legs and he whimpered. *Here comes the pain...* He thought. The punk teens swept Danny off his feet and ran away with him; leaving X and I to fight the old lady.

"I need to speak to the boy. Alone." She asserted with a heavy British accent. She was talking to X.

"No." He retorted bluntly. The woman squinted at Xavier as if she couldn't see him. Her eyes widened briefly when she recognized who X really was.

"Well, if it isn't Prince Drahc'ir. You couldn't have chosen a better hologram? I can see right through it. Never mind that. Like I said, I need to speak to the boy." Electric sparks danced from the woman's fingers as she spoke. Two surges of electricity bolted from them and seized Xavier; causing him excruciating pain. He bellowed in anguish. "And it wasn't a request this time. You may be a prince on Chorifer, but you're on Earth now. Your royal lineage means nothing here, I'm afraid."

The electricity was coursing through Xavier's body; boiling his blood. He was breathless and speechless. After about 30 seconds of this torture, X blacked out and the woman released him; turning her sights to me.

"Now, tell me, love: who does your father work for?"

I was flabbergasted. "Um, madam," I started, politely in light of the situation. "My father is dead. He has been for some time now."

"Are you not Franklin Josiah Lamberg?"

"Yeah, that's me…" I replied, mildly freaked out.

"Is your mother not Elizabeth Rae Lamberg?" she asked again.

"Yeah, how'd you know that?"

"And your father, is he not Isaiah Franklin Lamberg?" I nodded. Someone's been doing their research.

"Then, foolish boy, your father is very much alive and he's meddling in affairs that do not concern him." The elderly woman grabbed me by the neck and raised me in the air with surprising ability considering her age and condition. "Now, I'll only ask you once more: who does your father work for?"

Hannah and the Moroccan teleporter reappeared in the parking lot. She fell to her knees when they landed. The man was stout and stood at 5'4 but what he lacked in height, he made up for in muscle. The Moroccan man lifted Hannah by her arms.

"I'm sorry for this, young one but you're an obstacle in our way of greatness." The old, buff Moroccan head butted Hannah sharply and tossed her into a nearby, topless gray convertible. She landed in the driver's seat.

Hannah shook off the blow and realized the key was still in the ignition. She smiled and turned the key. The car started immediately and the engine purred smoothly. Hannah shifted into drive, pulled out of the parking spot, and jammed down on the accelerator. She rammed into her attacker (who was caught off guard) as hard as she could and he hurtled through the air but teleported to safety before he hit the ground; and by "safety" I mean the passenger seat of the car Hannah was in.

"Where are we going, young one? You look so young. Do you even have a driver's license?" the Moroccan elbowed Hannah in the face and blood dripped from her mouth. "Child, that was a very mean thing for you to do. You see, now I'm gonna have to kill you." Hannah wiped the blood from her face.

"You'll have to find me first." She taunted and vanished from sight. All that could be seen was the driver's side door (of the moving car) open and shut. Then, the sound of Hannah hitting the ground, rolling, was heard. Her footsteps echoed back to the Moroccan as she pounded the pavement back to the park.

"Hm, looks like I have myself a runner." He said then he teleported after her.

Sarita was sure she would split her head open or worse on impact, but she didn't panic. Instead, she focused on her projected landing and, with a flip of her wrist, the area grew to resemble a dense grassland. Sarita landed harmlessly in the overgrown weeds by the hill where Hannah and Curt were infected and looked for her suitors. They had crept up, silently, behind her.

"Honey," the wife began, which startled Sarita. "Maybe we should keep this one. She's special." The wife grinned at Sarita and pinched her cheeks.

"Pumpkin, that wasn't the plan. But, I tell you what: when this is over, I'll get you a puppy." The husband offered.

"Can we name it peaches?" She asked.

"You can name it whatever you want." He said.

"I love you, baby." She admitted.

"Love you too, babe." Sarita was beyond confused at this point.

"Um, excuse me, Mr. and Mrs. Freakshow," said Sarita. "Can I go now?" The newly weds turned to look at her, still holding hands.

"I'm sorry, little girl," the husband explained. "But the only place you'll be going is six feet under."

"Oh, um, good to know." Sarita was being sarcastic.

"Sweetie," the wife interrupted, "What kinda puppy will we get?"

"Dunno, a good one?" he said.

"What kind?" she wondered.

"What kinds are there?" he asked. While the two talked, Sarita was coming up with a plan. With her hands behind her back, using her index fingers, Sarita summoned two, thick tree roots, one on her left and right side. The roots wrapped around Sarita's waist like a belt and raised her over the heads of the couple, then placed her behind them.

When the married couple realized she moved, they turned around as one, instead of individually. The two would not let go of each other's hand.

"Interesting." Sarita whispered.

She had a plan but she'd need some more time and a little help. The newly weds were about to attack again when Sarita shot both hands in the air and immediately all the vegetation within a hundred foot radius grew wildly. It was now a massive grassy jungle. Sarita used the growth as a distraction and took off in the direction of the picnic area. You could hear her pushing through the tall grass. The wife fumed, realizing they had lost their prey.

"Ugh. Honey, when we get a puppy, we're gonna need a leash."

The rabid rabbit charged Chris at full speed. Chris pounded his fist on the ground and a series of stone walls appeared between him and the approaching onslaught. The rabbit, running on his hind legs, ripped through each barrier with his razor sharp claws. Chris created more obstacles for the beast but none worked. The rabbit slashed Chris across the chest, leaving bloody gashes and staining his yellow polo shirt dark red.

"Ah!" Chris cried in pain.

He tried to check his wounds but they were sensitive to the touch.

Chris exhaled jaggedly. He willed stone spikes to form from his wrists and sent them flying towards the rabbit. Chris hit his target in the neck and abdomen; causing the rabbit to stumble backwards. Thinking fast, Chris slammed his open palms together and the vibrations from it created a pit behind the mammal; which the rabbit quickly fell into. Chris made a fist with both hands and horizontal bars of clay closed the pit after the rabbit; creating a make shift jail cell.

Chris rose, wobbly, to his feet and limped to the imprisoned animal. It was roaring like a lunatic and shaking the bars violently and the bars weren't going to take much more abuse.

The little girl, who was standing off to the side, was giggling.

"Fluffy hates cages. They make him…crazy." She said. As she spoke, the rabbit busted through the bars and out of his hole. When he landed, the earth shook. He had grown in size since Chris last saw him. It had a mad look in its eyes; not mad as in angry, mad as in mentally unstable.

The rabbit pulled the stone spikes from his neck and stomach, and when he did, some cotton stuffing slipped out from the openings.

"What?" Chris wondered.

"Oh. Oh! Fluffy is my stuffed animal. He's not real. But he's still my best friend. And with the help of my power, we can play all day!" the girl exclaimed. The rabbit's wounds stitched themselves up as if they never happened. He was now fully healed and more than ready for the next match. "Sooooo," The girl grinned. "You have two choices: either you play with me, or I let Fluffy play with you. And as you have seen, Fluffy plays rough."

Danny had had all he could take of the emo mob steering him against his will.

"You know," he said as they bounced along. "As much fun as this sausage fest is, I think I'll be leaving now."

Danny morphed into a gray humpback whale; crushing about 90% of the copies. And when each copy died, they made a sound similar to that of a balloon popping and vanished in a cloud of smoke.

The remaining 20 punk teens regrouped then pounced on Danny; pummeling him with a fury of punches, kicks, bites, and scratches. Danny was defenseless in his present form so, after a minute or two of getting jumped, he shifted into a beige field mouse and discreetly slipped between the legs of the preoccupied teens.

It didn't take long for the punk teens to realize Danny was gone but, by the time they did, he had already changed into a silverback gorilla and taken the offensive position in this fight. Danny, in gorilla form, was swinging his fists wildly; smacking clone after clone out of existence.

After a few attempts, Danny lucked out and hit the original punk teenager. He knocked the punk teen off his feet and all the leftover doppelgangers disappeared. Danny returned to his human self and put his clothes back on.

"See?" he said, winded. "You're all talk. Don't mess with Danny. I'll lay you out!" the teen was ignoring Danny's boasting. He had felt something crack when he fell and realized what it was. The punk teen's MP3 player was smashed to pieces in his pocket. He was so pissed that he couldn't speak.

"You Retard!" he erupted, finally. "My tunes are trashed!"

He showed Danny the shattered pieces.

"Oh, my bad, bro." Danny said, sheepishly.

"Your bad? Your bad?!" The punk teen seethed.

"What if I add an 'I'm sorry'?" The punk teen put the chucks of electronics in his pocket once again and sent Danny the coldest stare possible.

"If I mess with you, you'll lay me out? Really? Let's test that." The teen emitted a primitive howl and hundreds of clones stemmed from him, then more sprouted from the first batch of clones. By the end, there were about 5,000 copies; Danny was incredibly outnumbered. But he had an idea.

"You think you can lay us all out?!" The clones echoed.

"Honestly," Danny began. "I don't think I can. But, like some wise guy in the past once said: 'If you can't beat 'em, join 'em.'"

Danny winked in the general direction of the clones and transformed into a carbon copy of the punk teen. After the change was complete, Danny charged at the crowd; knocking over a handful of clones and successfully disappearing into the mob. As the punk teens searched for the odd man out, Danny couldn't help but think: *Dude, I'm a friggin' genius.*

The elderly British woman's grip on my neck was steadily growing tighter and I was swaying in and out of consciousness.

"Oh, knickers. I don't want to kill the boy. Not yet, anyway." She promptly released me and I gasped for air. "Make my life easy and tell me who your father works for! I searched out your little group because I knew he'd contact you. He must've. Don't lie to me!"

A rope made of pure electricity jolted from her palm and wrapped itself around my neck. *Out of the frying pan and into the fire.* I thought. The pain was indescribable at first, but after a while, I went numb. Not that she stopped her assault; it's just that the voltage was so high that my nerves couldn't register it all.

"Look. Nut job. I don't know what you think you know, but, to my knowledge, my dad is dead. And even if he's not, he hasn't talked to me in…forever. So, just back off!" A fiery force field emanated from my body, repelled the electric chain, and tried to burn the woman; who countered with an electric field of her own.

"Oh? We have a pyrokinetic on our hands?" She asked, intrigued.

"No. No. No. I dunno how I did that. I swear."

"Again with the lying. Liars don't make friends."

A twisted and evil smile crept across the woman's face but was washed away in an instant. A dark red stain appeared on her once pearl white t-shirt and spread to canvas the whole garment. She was bleeding. Badly. More importantly, she was dying.

The elderly woman crumbled to her knees, then fell flat on her face and she just laid there; painting the dead grass beneath her an odd tone of crimson. Behind her, stood Xavier; wielding a bloody dagger. (Obviously the murder weapon.)

"Dude!" I squealed, reeling with shock. "You effing killed her!"

"Of course I killed her! You obviously weren't going to!" X threw the dagger to the ground and it stuck in the soil; blade first. He got in my face and grabbed me by the shirt collar.

With X this close to me, I noticed something weird: the whites of eyes were purple and his pupils were a bright yellow.

"This isn't a game! It's survival of the fittest!" X squinted at me and leaned in alittle closer then whispered: "Kill or be killed." He abruptly released me, went to the woman's lifeless body, grabbed the emerald pentagonal medallion and put it around his neck.

"Let's go." He said to me, annoyed. "That was pathetic. 'I dunno how I did that. It swear.'" X turned his head to look at me. "Well, you had better learn how. And fast." X then walked away and as he did, the corpse of the British woman decomposed into a pile of sand and blew straight into the sky. So, to recap, I'm best friends with a bipolar, murderous alien and a dead body turned into sand and flew off into space. It was at that moment that I realized I might have been in over my head.

Across the park, the minions of the elderly British woman disappeared in the same manner that she did; leaving my friends stunned and confused. The sun was setting and everyone was pretty tired. We gathered in the parking lot when everything died down. No pun intended.

"Dude, what was that?" Danny protested. "I was about to pwn some punk rocker clones back to the Stone Age."

"Shut up, Danny." I stated, cutting off his rant and began to quote X. "This isn't a game. It's survival of the fittest. Kill or be killed." I paused. "We need to train. Master our abilities…"

"You mean WE need to train." Chris interrupted. "You don't have any powers, remember?"

"What are you talking about? Of course I do." I defended.

"Then, prove it." He said.

"Now?" I asked.

"Now." He replied.

I looked to the horizon. The sun was only partially visible. It would be dark soon.

"It'll be dark soon." I said aloud. "Some other time. Besides, there are more important things at hand." I stalled; Chris wasn't swayed.

"No. No more excuses. Prove you have a power. Right now." He demanded.

"Hey, chill out, Alexander the Great. We're all friends here." Danny said, trying to mediate.

Oh, and for the benefit of the uneducated, Alexander the Great was gay. So, the joke made sense. (Cuz everyone called Chris gay.) Ok. Back to the story.

Danny's words calmed Chris down a bit and the whole thing woulda blown over if I hadn't put my foot in my mouth.

"No, Danny. It's fine. If Chris wants proof, I'll give him proof. Tomorrow. 9 PM. Your house, Chris. I'll be there."

Dang it. I hated losing and being called out, so, what else could I have done? Oh yeah. I coulda shut up and brushed it off.

"Alright. Tomorrow. My place. See you then, *buddy*." Chris said with emphasis on buddy. I suddenly felt sick. Everyone hopped in their various vehicles and went home shortly after the engagement was set. Except for me. I had a few things weighing heavily on my mind. How was I gonna get control of powers that I didn't have? I had 24 hours or so to figure that out. But what was bothering me the most was what the British wom-

woman had said. How could my dad be alive? And if he was, where was he? Ugh. I needed a break.

Meanwhile, as my friends and I were fighting for our lives in the park, Brody and his friends were hanging out. But it wasn't leisurely hanging. I guess it could've been called a meeting of sorts.

Brody's friends Timmy and Carrie (from the community pool) arrived first. Brody was on his couch, watching some trashy reality TV show when the doorbell rang. At the door, there was a very skinny Caucasian girl standing at about 5'5. Her hair was light brown, almost dirty blonde with greenish brown eyes that had a calming effect when you stared directly into them.

"Hey, Carrie." Brody said and he leaned in for a hug. They embraced but Carrie squeezed a bit too hard and lifted Brody a few feet off the ground. Oh, I kinda forgot to mention that Carrie developed super strength from the pool incident.

"Carrie…" Brody whispered, breathlessly. "You're hugging to tight."

"Oh," she said and released him. "Sorry." She said, embarrassed.

"It's cool." He played it off. "Come in. Where's Timmy?" Carrie looked back.

"Um, I dunno. He was right behind-" As if on cue, Timmy, carried by hundreds of Red Robins, fluttered to the ground. Each bird was grasping some part of Timmy's clothing with his or her talons. Timmy said something to them that was indecipherable, consisting of chirps and tweets, but the birds understood. They released their grip after Timmy's feet touched the cement and flew off in different directions.

"Thanks, guys." He called to them in English.

Timmy was about 5'11 or 6'0 without shoes on, but his shoes added an inch or two. Although Timmy was white, he always had a bronzeish tan about him. His eyes were dark brown but whenever his light brown hair was in his face, his eyes appeared to be black.

"You swear that you're Sofa King cool." Carrie sneered, "But in reality, you're not."

Timmy gave Carrie a cheesy grin, showing his braces.

"Love you too, Carrie." Timmy had gained an ability from the meteor as well. He could now speak any language, including animal languages.

"What are we doing here, Brody?" Carrie inquired when they had entered Brody's living room and plopped down on his soft couch.

"Oh. Yeah. That." Brody paused. "That's...a long story." Brody proceeded to fill his friends in on everything. And I mean everything. He held back no info.

"Whoa." Carrie mumbled and sank into the sofa. "Aliens? That's too science fiction for my taste."

"Yeah, well, it's true. And my friends can use all the help they can get." The doorbell rang at the end of Brody's sentence; almost as if it was planned. "Perfect timing." He remarked and shot for the door.

Brody returned quickly, with two guests at his side. Timmy's eyes brightened when he recognized the two.

"Ey! Rick, Alexis, what's up?"

Rick Lorette stood at about 6'2 and had piercing blue eyes with dark blonde hair that was short and mildly unkempt. Rick smiled at Timmy and game him a sorta half wave (he raised his open palm and tilted his hand to the left a bit).

The first things people notice about Alexis Cooker are her eyes. They're a very light hazel and have a fiery glow to them; which fits her personality well. Alexis was only about 5'6 but she wasn't scared of anyone. She had blonde hair that was parted down the middle that day, with a few strands tucked behind her ears so she could see.

"Hey, Timmy." Alexis said with a radiant smile. The two new editions to the group took seats on the armrests of the couch and waited for some sort of instruction.

"Ok. So, I called you all here because we all have new-found 'Talents'. For those of you who don't know, Carrie has super strength, Timmy speaks to animals and is fluent in every language known to man, Rick can grow/shrink to any size, Alex has super speed, and anything I say comes true. We were given these gifts for a reason-"

"What is that reason?" asked Rick, interrupting Brody's speech.

"I...uh, I dunno." He replied dumbly. The doorbell rang once again. "This has gotta be someone who can shred some light on this situation..." He said under his breath as he went to answer the door.

The man on the other side of the door was not someone Brody had ever expected to see again. Brody's face flushed chalk white as if he had seen a ghost. Although, in his mind, he did.

Brody's knees began to shake and his voice trembled and he said, "Dude, what are you doing here?! You're dead..."

Chapter 8

"Isolation"

Isolation: The act of an individual being socially withdrawn or

removed from society.

It was a new day but nothing had changed. I awoke that morning hoping that somehow yesterday was a dream; that the past few months were just a dream. But they weren't. I was still screwed come 9 p.m.

Actually, I'm using the wrong tense. That morning was this morning. I was supposed to meet Chris tonight and make a fool of myself. But instead, I'm about to die. I may have misjudged which situation was the lesser of two evils. But I'm getting ahead of myself. Again. Let me explain exactly how I got here. This present nightmare all started with a simple dare that went horribly wrong.

While I valiantly tried to discover my ability, Danny and Sarita were loitering in front of a local convenience store, slurping on icy drinks. They sat like this for a while until the sun began to set on the rolling hills in the distance; casting a shadow on the Remington Estate. Oh, as a side note, the Remington Estate is the house that on fire right now.

Sarita noticed that the Remington Estate's shadow was shaped like a ghost and remembered something.

"Hey, Danny." He looked up at her upon hearing his name.

"Mhmm?" He mumbled, still sipping.

"Ya know the Remington house is haunted by Old man Remington's dead wife, right?"

"Nuh uh," Danny argued, "Is it really?"

Sarita nodded, answering Danny's question.

"Look." She pointed at the shadow. "They say if you go in around sunset, you can actually see her in the kitchen, where she died, cooking breakfast for her husband."

Danny choked on his drink and started hacking to clear his throat. "Ok. Now I know you're lying." He said, after he could breathe again.

"Oh yeah? Prove me wrong. Go up there."

Danny took a last gulp of his drink and threw it away.

"Fine, I will." He said then shape shifted into a pigeon and flew towards the mansion, leaving his clothes in a pile next to Sarita. He looked back and could vaguely make out Sarita smiling; waving with one hand and giving him the "thumbs up" sign with the other.

"Retard." Sarita said under her breath. This wasn't Sarita. As soon as Danny was out of sight, the imposter pretending to be Sarita revealed her true form: it was really Jayden. It appears that her power allows her to mimic other people's abilities and she had just used Danny's against him.

From inside the convenience store, Derrick emerged with a soda of his own.

"Did he fall for it?" Derrick asked Jayden.

"Yes, Prince Sivart, he did." Derrick grinned and sipped his drink.

"Good." He pulled out his cell phone, created a new text message, and sent it to X. "Let's go, my little copy cat." Derrick said after he returned the phone to his pocket. "We've got work to do."

Xavier received Derrick's text a few minutes after it was sent. It read: *I did my part. Now, it's your turn.* X read this and knew exactly what he had to do. He closed the message and started dialing a number...

I was about to give up trying to get my power to work. It was already 7:45 PM; I only had alittle over an hour left. I had lost all hope of avoiding humiliation …when my phone rang. I looked at the caller ID and it was X.

"Hey, X." I said, discouragingly.

"I know about your problem," He said, bluntly; skipping the pleasantries. "Meet me at the Remington Estate. I know how to help. I'll leave the door open. Come now." Click. The line was dead shortly after X's last word. I guess I had no choice. I grabbed my jacket and car keys and headed out.

Danny perched himself on the Remington Estate front gate at 7:45 p.m. Behind the gate, there was a long and winding road that ended at the mansion door. The mansion itself covered about an acre of land and was two stories high. The estate was centuries old and worn down by decades of hard rains and heavy winds. Two massive stone pillars supported the covering over the porch steps. The entire front of the mansion was decorated with large windows; foggy with the dirt of never being cleaned and the house was an off white color with paint chipping in various places. Basically, it wasn't that great of a place to start with and it could very well be haunted. Especially with its overgrown lawn that was harboring who knows what kind of creatures.

Danny flew to the porch and landed on the front step. He changed back to his normal form and realized he left his clothes at the convenience store. Danny crouched down and hid behind one of the stone pillars to shield his nakedness. *How am I gonna get in here?* He thought.

Danny mulled the situation over and came up with an elaborate plan to accomplish his mission when he realized…he never tried the door. He stood up, covering his private areas and jiggled the handle. It was unlocked. *How embarrassing.* He thought and swung the door open.

It was dusty and dark except for the dim glow of a candle on the nightstand by the door. Danny picked up the candle and journeyed deeper into the dark abyss that was the Remington estate. He treaded softly because the candle barely illuminated a foot in front of him.

Danny stumbled on various unseen objects on his way to the kitchen and was burned by dripping, hot wax every step or two. He found the kitchen with less effort than he expected. The inside of old man Remington's kitchen had a bit of an Amish feel to it. The cabinets were completely wooden and the hinges were rusted. The oven was on an island in the middle of the room, no stovetop. The sink was made of frail aluminum and when too many dishes were in the sink, it would get dents under the pressure; it was off at the left corner of the room. There was no fridge; just a mini icebox without ice and it was full of expired food because of this. The icebox was positioned on the counter next to the sink and there was a window right above it that led outdoors. Danny felt on the wall for a light switch. He found it and flipped it up. The light flickered then exploded; sending sparks and glass shards everywhere.

Great. Danny thought. He continued through the kitchen and noticed something: there was no ghost. *Ha.* He thought. *I knew it. Wait til I tell Sarita. ugh. I forgot to bet her that she was wrong.* Danny was about to leave, satisfied with his findings, when he heard a meowing sound coming from the kitchen's island.

It was Mr. Jinxie. He was sitting on his hind legs, swishing his tail back and forth. Next to him, there was a large cup of vegetable oil; probably old and stagnant. Danny and Mr. Jinxie locked eyes.

"Don't. You. Dare." Danny threatened. The suicidal cat had a mischievous gleam in his eyes and, with a strong swing of his tail, Mr. Jinxie toppled the oil cup; spilling it all over the counter and onto the floor.

"Ugh. Cats like you are the reason I used to shoot animals with my slingshot, growing up." Danny scowled and searched the cabinets, candle still in hand, for paper towels.

After he had checked 5 or 6 cabinets, Danny found some ancient napkins that make a strange crunching sound as he used them.

"Better than nothing." He reasoned and began to clean up the mess; napkins in his left hand, candle in his right.

Danny had created a pile of used, oily napkins on the counter of the island (which he had planned to take out with him) and was almost done when…

"Hello? X, you in here?" I called from the front door of the house, startling Danny. Shocked by the sound of my voice, Danny jumped and made he biggest mistake ever: he dropped the candle. This wouldn't have been so bad if the candle hadn't landed on the oil soaked napkins, which ignited on contact.

"Oh Dang! Fire!" Danny screamed.

A frightened Mr. Jinxie saw the flames and instinctively leaped out the window to safety; knocking the icebox off the counter, spilling its spoiled contents onto the floor.

"You're a genius, Suicidal Sammy!" Danny concluded; realizing the fire was too large to contain and ran towards the window to escape but slipped on the water from the icebox. Danny hit the ground with a slam and just laid like this. There he was, lying on his back in pain, naked, and in a fire that he caused, in a house that wasn't his, with footsteps rapidly approaching. Danny was not having a good day. But he had more pressing matters at hand: he didn't know who was coming and Danny needed to hide. He only had one option…

*****

I pulled up to the Remington Estate Gate at 8:00ish. I sat behind the wheel for a second; mentally preparing myself for whatever mumbo jumbo mind games Xavier had in mind for me.

I climbed out of my car and shook the gate: locked. *Lucky me.* I thought. I am not a climber. I don't do athletics in general. It woulda been easy if this was a chain link fence, but it was a 15 foot gate with iron bars; iron bars…that were spaced pretty far apart. Being the lanky kid I was, I knew what I was gonna do.

I found the widest gap in the bars and began to squeeze through. I got wedged halfway through. *Man, I shouldn't have eaten so much.* I thought. I sucked in my newly formed gut and slid through. Frankie: one, Gate: zero.

I walked up the driveway to the door and knocked. I don't know why I did that: I knew no one was home. I jiggled the door handle and the door creaked open. It was really dark and the only light source came from an insignificant glow in the distance.

"Who is that?" I whispered. "Hello? X, you in here?" I called from the front door.

There was no reply for a moment, then: "Oh Dang! Fire!" could be heard. The voice sounded so familiar.

I know it wasn't the most intelligent thing I've ever done, but I ran blindly into the dark to see what was wrong.

The voice had come from the kitchen but when I arrived, all I saw was a spilled mini icebox, a large grease fire, and Mr. Jinxie. Of course he'd be there.

"What are you doing here, Suicidal Sammy?" The cat just stared at me and limped towards me, purring. Why was he limping? The wooden cabinets were up in flames and out of control. The kitchen was consumed in seconds and I had to go before the whole house did the same, so I grabbed the cat and ran for the exit.

The firefighters could be heard blaring their sirens as they rushed to put out the fire…

*****

So, that's my story to this point and time. I wish it wouldn't end like this but what can I do? I can't control or even use my power. I was surrounded by fire, Mr. Jinxie was being a serious pain in my a…rm, and the ceiling was crumbling. I remember my last thought being: *I swear, Mr. Jinxie, if we survive this, you're getting neutered.* And after that, the ceiling came down on me.

Meanwhile, in Chris's room, there was a small gathering of my friends anticipating my arrival. Boy, would they be disappointed.

"It's 9:00. Where is he?" Chris asked Sarita, impatiently. Chris and I weren't exactly "Friends". We just sorta hung out with the same people so we were forced to tolerate each other. Not that we hate each other, we just don't like each other. "Probably chickened out. I knew he had no powers."

"Shut up, Chris!" Hannah exploded. "Why do you have to be so...hurtful? You two have got to work together; now more than ever. Its just you, me, Frankie, Sarita and Dan-where is Danny?" Hannah wondered.

"I dunno," Sarita answered. "He was *supposed* to meet me at Joe's corner store but never showed."

"Whatever." Chris brushed off their comments and turned on the T.V. There was an urgent news bulletin.

"If you're just now joining us, we're live, covering the incineration of the Remington Estate," The female news reporter began. "Earlier this evening, neighbors reported seeing smoke and called the local authorities. There's no clear sign of the cause of the blaze but eye witnesses say they saw these two boys..." Two police sketches of Danny and me were posted on the screen. "Enter the house shortly before the fire started. It is unknown whether or not the two teens made it out in time. But what we do know is, that if the boys aren't out by now, there's no hope of them ever coming back out alive. Our condolences go out to the parents of the boys. If anyone knows any information on the identity of the boys, please call the station. There may be a reward. In other news..."

Chris shut off the T.V. and my three friends sat in silence as they let the info sink in. Their faces were devoid of emotion. Chris's room remained eerily quiet until Chris broke the silence.

His head hung low and he didn't turn to face the girls when he asked: "What do we do now?" Immediately after, Sarita busted into tears and, as if responding to her sadness, it began to rain...

*****

The rain was steady but not strong enough to extinguish the burning home. At the Remington Estate Gate, lost in a sea of reporters, cameramen, and firefighters, there were two familiar faces.

"This was a risky plan, Drahc'ir. You could lose two of your humans tonight. And for what? To unlock one of their powers? Pathetic. You knew that boy would have power trouble. You were born with the gift of foresight, for Kire's sake! How do you even know they're still alive?" Derrick asked.

"It's simple, Sivart," X replied. "If they were dead, I'd be in Limbo, waiting for the death bringer and you'd have my medallions." X lifted his medallions up and waved them in Derrick's face. "Oh, look. I'm still here and so are my medallions. Guess you know what that means." X stated, condescendingly. Derrick batted the medallions away and scoffed.

"Whatever. I'm leaving. But before I do, promise me something." Derrick said.

"Yeah? What do you want?"

"I want to fight you. No more distractions. No more stalling. I want to end this. Now. You shouldn't even be here." Derrick said coldly. "I'd hate to sentence my own brother to death but you knew that it would come to this eventually." He explained. The rain was harder now. The reporters began to abandon the story and the firefighters decided to let the fire burn itself out.

Eventually, it was just X and Derrick: having a stand off in the rain. Good versus Evil. The fierce downpour was soaking the brothers but they didn't move. Lightning cracked, illuminating the sky a brief moment, and thunder bellowed after but the two were motionless. Locked in a face off. Neither one blinked.

When X didn't reply, Derrick added: "So? Do we have a deal?" Xavier nodded then extended his hand. Bathed in the bright glow of the mansion's flames, in between lightning strikes, the alien siblings stood, in the rain, shaking hands. This act sealed the deal to a wager that would inevitably lead to one of their untimely demises.

Chapter 9

"Ignition"

Ignition: To subject to fire or intense heat; to start

As the portion of the ceiling was crumbling down, time seemed to slow to a crawl. I saw the flames flickering and swaying in slow motion. Rain dripped through the cracks, drop-by-drop.

Suddenly, everything went white and the room went silent, as if someone had hit the "mute" button. *Am I dead?* I thought. *No, I can't be. I can still hear my heartbeat.* Thump-thump. Thump-thump. It was beating steadily.

Dying is a strange feeling. I thought you were supposed to be, I don't know, cold or something. But I wasn't. A force inside me erupted and it was hot. If this makes any sense, my soul felt like it was on fire. My pulse quickened and my vision returned. Time sped back to normal and I unleashed something amazing. Shocked back into reality, I inhaled deeply and, when I exhaled, white-hot flames exploded from every pore on my body, but didn't burn my clothes. The pure white flames blasted the debris that I was buried under into hundreds of pieces and the fire spread throughout the house; expunging the flames of the burning home from existence. I concentrated on manipulating my flames and they returned to me.

"Whoa!" Mr. Jinxie said. *Wait.* He doesn't talk. The cat hopped from my arms and transformed into a familiar face. It was Danny; a very naked Danny.

"Whoa. Two hands there, buddy. You're nude." I said and he covered up.

84

"Dude, that was so bad A. How'd you do that?!"

I shrugged. "I dunno. I just thought about it and it happened." To demonstrate, I raised my left hand, thought about it, and it was engulfed in the white flames seconds later. Danny was hyped beyond belief.

"That's amazing! You have like the coolest power. Hands down." I smiled. I guess I did.

"So, what do we do now?" I asked him, clueless.

"Duh, fool. You flaunt it. To Chris' house!" he exclaimed and, after changing into a black raven, he flew off into the night sky. *We gotta get that kid some clothes that will actually stay on.* I thought.

I dusted myself off and walked out the burnt door, closing it behind me; not that it would do any good. I squeezed back out the gate the same way I came in and went to my car. There was a note under my windshield wiper and a package on the hood. The note read:

I'm so proud of you, son! A pyrokinetic? Very impressive. Burning down mansions? Not so impressive. But you'll get better. With practice. I wish I could have given you this in person but it's still too dangerous for us to meet. Don't look for me. When the time is right, I'll come to you. P.S. the package is for your shape-shifting friend. They'll help with his little wardrobe malfunctions.

– Dad

A wide range of emotions darted through my mind: Happiness, sadness, bewilderment and then...nothing. I decided I wasn't going to worry about him until I see him. And who knows when that'll be? At that moment, I was worried about other things. Like Derrick and my friends that he had under his spell. With that in mind, I completely forgot about my dad, grabbed Danny's package, hopped in my car, and headed to Chris' house; hoping that everyone wasn't getting impatient.

*****

Sarita and the others had calmed down a bit by now. Sarita, especially.

"Guys. Guys. Wait. Remember yesterday?" she inquired after wiping her tears. "That British chick from the park?"

"The one Xavier killed?" Hannah added.

"Um, yeah. When she died and dissolved into sand, her whole team disappeared with her. But we're still here. Xavier said if one dies, we all do." Sarita concluded.

"Well, two died. Maybe the rules are different." Chris suggested.

"Can we stop saying 'died'? Respect the deceased. Please." Hannah said weakly.

"Excuse us," Danny and I interrupted as we walked into Danny's room. "But I think we should get a say on who's deceased and who's not." I explained.

"Yeah, dude. Respect the wishes of the undead." Danny joked. Sarita and Hannah flew over and hugged the crap out of us.

"We thought you were dead!" Sarita exclaimed.

"Yeah. We gathered that much." I said.

"I'm, uh, glad you're not dead, flames." Chris said, sheepishly.

"Yeah. Me too." I replied.

For those of you who don't speak "guy" fluently, here's a translation of what Chris said: "If you would've died, I would've missed you. So, I'm happy you're alive. Sorry I was a dilweed before. Let's be friends." Ok. Ok. I may have exaggerated a little on the last part but I got the meaning.

"Ok. So, everyone's well and good. But where do we go from here?" Chris asked to no one in particular.

"Now," replied X as he appeared in Chris' doorway. "You train."

"Wow. I love how no one even knocks anymore. Does no one know what a doorbell is?" Chris muttered.

I was a bit weary to trust X again, seeing as how he had set me up to get burned. Literally. But I did get my powers be-

cause of it…and X is always right. So, I had no other option besides going along with Xavier's suggestion, but I'd be watching
him.

"X is right. Tomorrow, we practice." I said.

And with no opposition, we called it a night.

I awoke the next morning in a blindly white room, not
remembering how I got there. The floor was hard and the room
smelled vaguely like bleach. The walls were bare and the only
thing I could hear was the steady buzzing of the fluorescent
lights overhead. There was no visible exit.

"How did I get here?" I asked aloud.

"I drugged you, Frankie." X explained. Yeah, that's
strike one for X. "I had to do it. I did the same to the rest of the
Phalanx. You all needed to practice in my indestructible facili-
ties but I couldn't let you know where it was." X looked shamed
by his actions. "I…still need my secrets, you know?" I nodded
slowly and Xavier changed the subject. "Your other friends are
training in groups of two but since there's an odd number, you'll
be training with me." That was fine with me. I could use all the
help I could get.

"What do I have to do?" I asked.

"Well, first, show me what you can do already." He said.
So, I showed him. I started with my hand and worked my way
around the rest of my body until I was covered head to toe in
self-induced flames. Fireballs formed in the palms of my hands,
suspended in midair. I sent the spheres rocketing towards X, nar-
rowing missing him.

"My bad. That wasn't intentional." I lied.

"I see you can use your power. But can you *control* it?"
To answer his question, I concentrated and the fireballs returned
to my hands and I extinguished them. X was impressed. "Excellent work. Now, let's see your lightning."

*****

"Ok. Ok. Gimme another animal." An excited Danny
begged of Sarita as he changed back to his human form. Danny's
clothes were on the floor, but he wasn't naked. The gift from my

dad turned out to be some type of orange jumpsuit that didn't fall off when Danny changed shapes and it also was invisible whenever he morphed. So, he wouldn't be wearing clothes if he was an animal and he would be wearing clothes when he changed back.

"Turn into a bottlenose dolphin!" Sarita offered, jokingly but Danny thought she was serious.

"Ok. Coming up." Danny morphed into the light gray dolphin. It didn't take long for Danny to realize that there was no water in sight and dolphins didn't have lungs. He flopped around helplessly.

"You know I was kidding, right?" She asked, rhetorically.

"Obviously not." He replied between gasps. Danny changed back and inhaled deeply. "Gimme something realistic." He pleaded.

"Ok. Ok. Turn into…me."

"Be serious, Sarita."

"I am being serious. Have you ever tried that before?" He hadn't. Danny had never really practiced shifting into a human before except for once, at Lincoln Park. But there was no time like the present.

"Ok. Gimme a second." Danny memorized Sarita's physical features and gave it a shot. Danny's arm changed first. It grew shorter and skinnier, then it became darker. He entire body did the same. When Danny was finished, Sarita thought she was staring at herself in a mirror. He had become a carbon copy of his friend. Yup, the transformation was almost perfect. Except for one little thing.

"Wow. That's amazing, Danny. Say something."

Danny spoke and the words that came out sounded all wrong.

"Hi, I'm Sarita and I like boys?" Danny said in his own voice, not Sarita's. "How do I sound?" He asked her.

"Um, you sound like a man." She muttered.

"We'll have to work on that." Danny stated optimistically.

*****

"Where'd you go?" Chris asked in a seemingly empty room. Hannah had gone invisible and was testing how long she could stay that way. She had held it for 5 minutes when her left shoe reappeared. "There you go!" Chris noted and shot a spike near the lone foot, barely missing. "You've gotta hold it longer, Hannah. You've gotta focus. No offense, but you're kinda a one trick pony. If invisibility is all you've got, you need to master it."

"One trick pony?!" Hannah repeated, irritated. He shoe vanished again and Hannah teleported with a blindly flash of light (in the same manner as the Moroccan) and reappeared behind Chris. Hannah was visible now and, with a raised eyebrow, she said, "I'm a one trick pony, huh?"

Chris' jaw dropped. "How'd you do that?" he asked, puzzled.

"Teleporting is just another form of invisibility. 'Now you see me, now you don't.' It was an idea I had for a while and now I know for sure."

"When did you have time to think of this?" Chris inquired.

"Yesterday. What did you think I was doing before I came over to your house? Doing my nails?" Honestly, that's *exactly* what Chris thought. "Now, not to be demanding, but I think it's your turn, Chris." Hannah said with a smile that was meek yet arrogant.

*****

"Fool, what are you smokin'? What do you mean by 'Let's see your lightning?' I have fire, remember?"

I was beginning to think that X wasn't all there, mentally.

"Your abilities aren't limited to one skill." He explained. "It's true that your base ability is fire, but the possible variations

89

are only limited by your imagination. So…like I said, let's see your lightning."

"How?" I asked.

"Fire is a bit reckless. Uncontrolled. It's wild and un-tamed. It's the exact opposite of lightning. Lightning is much more precise and concentrated. Lightning strikes one place and wherever it lands, sheer devastation follows. You will need to focus and pick a target. It's much easier when you have motivation. A reason to fight. Good luck."

I wasn't going to stall this time. I buckled down and thought of something to motivate me. Right off the bat, I remembered my good friends Jared, Laura, Curt, Staci and Jayden. And my *ex* best friend Derrick who was holding their minds captive, bending them to his will. I thought about my dad, who I hadn't seen in years and I wondered who he worked for. I recalled the elderly English woman and her friends. *How many more people will die before this is all over?*

I had discovered my motivation. I wanted to save my friends and win the TBC.

The lightning happened suddenly and was gone in an instant. I knew what drove me to fight and when I focused on that, the lightning came all too easily. The golden bolt of electricity shot from my left palm and bashed an immense hole in X's wall. The edges of the hole were charred and a dark sable color.

X turned to look at me. I was expecting him to reprimand me for his destroyed wall but instead he said, "Well done. That was much faster than I anticipated."

"What about the wall?" I asked, still surprised that he wasn't mad.

"Don't worry about it. Look." He pointed to the wall. The damage was disappearing. The hole was shrinking, the burned material flaked off, and the pure white surface was revealed. The wall was blemish free in no time. *Whoa*, I thought.

"So, what's next?" I asked X.

"Nothing is next." He replied. "You've learned all that I have to teach you. You're ready for the application. Let us go get the others."

X walked to the wall I had blasted and he placed his hand on it. The wall glowed bright orange and an exit appeared. X passed through and I followed him, with the door vanishing behind us.

*****

"That was perfect!" Sarita exclaimed.

"Fool, I know!" Danny repeated in Sarita's voice. He had perfected his mimic technique. "What about you though?" Danny asked as he changed back to himself. "Don't you wanna practice?"

"Nah. I'm good. I had my fill of training when you didn't show up to hang out with me the other day. I'm not gonna lie, I was planning on hurting you for standing me up."

"I woulda been there if Jayden-" Danny paused. He still liked Jayden but he needed to grasp that they were enemies now. It was a hard pill to swallow.

"We're gonna save them, you know." Sarita assured him and put her hand on his shoulder. Danny looked at Sarita and smiled halfheartedly. She shared the same fake smile that he wore.

Sarita forced a full grin and said, "Everything will be alright."

"Do you really believe that?" Danny asked earnestly. His question caught Sarita off guard. There was an awkward silence and before she could answer, a door formed on one of the walls then X and I peered through.

"You guys ready?" I asked.

"Yeah. Let's go." Danny answered immediately. So, with Danny and Sarita by our side, we left and headed to Chris and Hannah's room.

*****

"You what?" Hannah was puzzled.

91

"I can dirt surf. It's...uh...much cooler that it sounds." Chris tried to explain. "Obviously I can't show you here but believe me when I say it's...it's awesome." Chris wasn't being very convincing but then again he wasn't the most persuasive of our group.

"I'll show you later or something." He said awkwardly.

"Ok. I'll hold you to that." Hannah said.

"Let's go, you two." X declared when we came to the two. "You are all ready for Derrick and his Legion. But first, rest." He said as we all filed into Chris and Hannah's room. "Computer, convert to bedroom mode." X commanded and the room erupted with life. The walls revolved 180 degrees to reveal a total of four beds, one on each wall. In the center of the room, the floor opened and a fifth bed rose from below. Off in the corner, a door formed and, above it, a sign reading *restroom* appeared.

"You have all you need to restore your energy. Now, sleep." No one was tired but we all past out because of the sedatives being blown into the room from the air vents. X drugged us. Again. I believe that's strike two. X dragged us to each of the beds, turned out the lights and left us to dream.

As I slept, I had a familiar dream. It had been a few months since I first had it, but the dream was hard to forget. It was the light/dark gardener dream. I tried to stay asleep long enough to see the end but, as the light/dark plants attacked each other, I woke up.

We all took turns with the showers then changed back into our old clothes, fresh from the wash, that were at our bedsides. No one knew what time it was or even what day.

X returned after we were all dressed.

"How was your sleep?" He asked.

"Drug induced. And yours?" Danny retorted. X brushed off the comment and converted the room back to a training area.

Out of nowhere, it hit me. This fight was the fight from my dream. We were the light plants. I was the dormant one. I now knew the meaning of it all. Better late than never, I guess.

X summoned six circular platforms that glowed with a violet light.

"These telepads will take us back to Earth." He said

"I wasn't aware that we ever *left* Earth." Sarita remarked.

X was unphased.

"Let us go." He continued. X led by example and stepped on one of the glowing circles. The violet light intensified and surrounded X then he was gone in a flash. The rest of us were unsure about following X but we didn't really have a choice in the matter. So, my friends and I stood on our respective platforms and vanished shortly after.

Everyone reappeared in a grassy meadow in the middle of nowhere with Jared, Laura, Curt, Jayden, Staci, and, of course, Derrick to welcome us.

"So glad you could make it, brother." Derrick laughed.

"This is where it ends." X replied, solemnly.

"Right you are. Goodbye, Drahc'ir." Derrick said.

Both sides stood facing each other. Light versus Dark. It's funny that, while I should have been worried that someone would die here today, I was much more preoccupied with the fact that I saw this coming. Sorta.

I looked around at the situation that was all too familiar and couldn't help thinking: *Déjà vu.*

Chapter 10

"Application"

Application: To put into operation or effect

Today was the day. Fight or flight. Well, no. That wasn't true. There would be *no* running away. Only one of the two teams would survive.

There was no talking. Neither side made a move. A gentle breeze blew across the meadow and the grass swayed in the wind. Seeing my friends again wasn't as I had imagined. I wished this meeting were on better terms. I looked at Derrick. He met my gaze and winked at me. This was all just a game to him. Derrick didn't care who lived or died. All of the years that Derrick and I were best friends washed away at that moment. Then I lost it. I blasted streams of fire toward him but Jared blocked the flames with a wall of water.

Derrick shook his head, disapprovingly.

"Patience, Frankie, patience. I'm the main course. Don't skip the appetizers. Jared, reacquaint yourself with Frankie." Jared nodded and lunged at me, toppling me backwards. Sarita rushed to my aid, but Derrick wasn't going to her interfere.

"Staci," Derrick said, responding to Sarita's movement. "Create the battlegrounds and let's get this show on road." Staci nodded and her eyes and hands began to glow an intense shade of cobalt...

As I rolled through the grassy meadow, with Jared's hands around my throat, I noticed something odd. The surrounding area began to wash away like a chalk drawing that has been soaked by a hose. The original environment was replaced by another. I don't know how it happened, but we were now on the deck of a yacht, in middle of the ocean; Just Jared and me. It was a fair and cloudless day here (wherever "here" was). The salty air stung my nostrils and I could feel the waves gently rocking the boat. *Is this real?* I wondered. As I took in the sights, Jared remained undeterred. He was straddling my chest, still trying to strangle me. I gotta hand it to the guy, he's dedicated.

I wasn't thinking too clearly (most likely due to the lack of oxygen to my brain) but I did gather that Jared wasn't screwing around; he really wanted me dead and I needed to free myself. And I did; the best way I knew how. Instead using my power (which would've been a good idea) I craned my neck to the best biting position possible and clamped down on Jared's right arm. He howled in agony and released his grip.

Taking advantage of the situation I flipped Jared off of me, sending him sliding across the deck, under the railing, and into the water. He hit the water with a painful sounding splash and sunk like a brick.

I started to worry about Jared's safety when he didn't re-surface immediately but I remembered something that made me worry for an entirely different reason: Jared manipulates water and I threw him into one of the largest bodies of water in the world. This wasn't one of my greatest moments, I'll admit.

A few minutes passed and I cautiously rose to my feet just to be knocked over again by a strong wave that appeared out of nowhere and slammed me against the railing opposite to where Jared fell overboard. I spit out the saltwater that I had in-haled from the ocean swell. I looked overhead to realize the sky was now ashen gray and the water grew more violent by the sec-ond. I knew, instantly, the source of the grim weather.

The yacht shook aggressively as the waves picked up and, in the distance, I witnessed something horrifying: an enor-mous white cap wave (200 feet high, at least) was approaching the boat swiftly. And on the crest of the wave, riding it like a pro surfer, stood Jared; looking more menacing than I ever thought possible. His wave would swallow the entire boat in a few seconds but I was too paralyzed with fear to brace myself. All I could do was hold my breath for as long as possible and hope it would be enough...

What am I doing? I thought. *Am I just gonna give up without a fight like a punk?* I wasn't about to go out like that. I had a plan but it was risky. I needed Jared to get a lot closer.

I overcame my crippling fear of the water, stood up, and focused on what inspired me to fight. The tips of my middle and pointer finger on my right hand began to give off vast amounts of static discharge. I concentrated harder as I held my right hand to my chest.

The wind screamed and the yacht creaked as Jared grew closer. Then his wave descended; preparing to crush my tiny vessel. I could finally see the whites of Jared's eyes and I knew this was my only shot. *Wound, not kill,* I thought as I extended my right arm, pointed my middle and pointer fingers at Jared's heart and a brilliant bolt of lightning emerged from the fingers and struck their target with the accuracy of a skilled archer.

Jared was no longer in control of the wave and was easily swept up by it. I would've celebrated the victory if the yacht hadn't abruptly capsized, throwing me overboard. But this was just the tip of the iceberg. There was still the colossal wave to deal with and I was pretty sure it wouldn't go quietly.

The water crashed down full force and whipped me around mercilessly underwater. All the spinning and flipping wildly was making me nauseous. The sea calmed down and I swam to the surface. The sky was clear again. The yacht was right side up now and an unconscious Jared had washed up on the deck.

I climbed the side ladder and checked Jared's vitals. His heart was beating and he was still breathing. That's good. I guess. But I still had to two problems: I didn't how to drive a yacht and if I did, I had no idea where to go...

*****

Hannah was having her own problems outside an abandoned house of mirrors. She had no clue how she got there but

96

she thought she was alone...until Curt stepped out of the front entrance.

"Ah. There you are!" Curt said in a surprisingly friendly manner. He was acting so kind that it disarmed Hannah.

"How are you?" She asked him, as if everything was normal again.

"I'm good...now that you're here."

Hannah was so elated to hear this that she ran to Curt for a hug but was stopped in her tracks by some unseen force. It was Curt. Using his telekinesis, he lifted Hannah, shakily, into the air.

"Um, yeah. No hugs. I kinda have to kill you."

This statement threw Hannah off.

"But...but...I'm your girlfriend." She stuttered.

"Yeah...no. That's over. We're over." He said bluntly.

Hannah's innocence was shattered. She was heartbroken and that was a new thing for her. A single tear rolled down her cheek and she...flipped out.

Hannah teleported free of Curt's hold and reappeared a few feet in front of him.

"That's unexpected." He said, surprised, then he retreated into the house of mirrors with a furious Hannah close behind.

Hannah had regained her composure by the time she was inside the building. She reasoned Curt could be anywhere and that it would be best to have the element of surprise on her side so she went invisible then journeyed deeper into the maze of mirrors.

"Hannah, baby," Curt called, "Where are you?"

Don't answer him. It's a trap, she thought.

"Even if you don't answer me, I can still hear you." He replied to her thoughts. Hannah had forgotten that Curt could read minds as well. She needed to be spontaneous to beat her ex.

Curt's face was now reflected on every mirror around her but she couldn't tell the difference between the original and the illusions. Improvising wasn't Hannah's strong suit but she'd have to pick it up quickly.

She began counting backwards from 100 in her mind to keep herself from thinking.

100, 99, 98, 97, 96...

"What are counting for, love?"

...91, 90, 89...

Then Hannah teleported behind the mirror Curt was standing near and pushed it over, hoping to hit him, not missing a number in the process.

...83, 82, 81...

"You missed, hon. I'm over here." Curt blurted out from a different spot, completely falling for Hannah's bait.

...76, 75, 74...

Hannah knew where Curt was now and, without a thought, she teleported right in front of him, still invisible, and kicked Curt square in the nuts with all her might before he could even react.

Curt squeaked and fell to his knees. Taking no chances, Hannah buried Curt under every mirror she could get her hands on. When she was done, Curt was heavily entombed and showed no sign of going anywhere anytime in the near future. And, although he was probably badly injured, he'd survive.

"Hannah..." Curt whispered weakly from the pile.

Hannah rolled her eyes and walked towards the exit.

Douche, she thought as she left.

*****

Danny found himself in an arena at a renaissance fair. He wasn't alone though. He was keeping himself company, if that makes any sense. It was Jayden. She was copying Danny's shape shifting again.

"So, I hear you do a dead-on impression of a friend of mine." Danny said as he approached the doppelganger.

In response, Jayden shifted into Sarita and answered, "You heard correctly" in Sarita's voice.

Application

"That's a neat trick." Danny stated, unimpressed. "Let me try." He said and then morphed into Jayden; only he took a few liberties with her figure. To be specific, he added a beer belly and some serious junk in Jayden's trunk. Danny struck a pose in his new form.

"I look *just* like you. It's like looking in a mirror, right?" he smirked. Danny knew it hit a nerve but two could play that game. Jayden changed into Danny again, with a few new additions. She gave him insane acne and the biggest man boobs imaginable.

Danny was livid. He transformed into a male African lion and charged at his look-a-like. Jayden easily evaded the attack and turned into a Black Panther. She roared ferociously then pounced on Danny; locking her jaws on the back of his neck.

Danny struggled to free himself but that only made her bite down harder. Thinking fast, he changed into a dragonfly and flew to safety. But his freedom was short lived when Jayden knocked him out of the air with one swipe of her paw.

As he hurdled towards the earth, Danny morphed again, this time into a longhorn and rammed Jayden head on; launching her into a near by horse stable. The horse within the stable whined when she landed then it settled down.

"I would just like to say that I would never hit a girl. However, since you are clearly a panther, you're fair game."

On the left side of the stables, there were several suits of tarnished armor and a few wooden lances. Seeing this gave Danny a brilliant idea.

He reverted to his natural form then walked over to Jayden. She, too, had changed back and was wiping hay from her clothes.

"Suit up," Danny told her as he pointed to the armor. "We're settling this. Now." Then he grabbed a horse by its reins, some armor, a lance and headed to the opposite of the field.

It wasn't until Danny was dressed and on the horse's back that he remembered he had never been on horseback. While his opponent, being the diverse person she was, had gone horseback riding every Sunday, since she was 11.

"I'm so dead..." Danny told his horse and it neighed in agreement. "Oh. Thanks for the vote of confidence."

Danny and his horse trotted into position and Jayden did the same. Before Danny could wish her luck, Jayden sprinted towards him without warning. Danny jammed his helmet on and met Jayden's speed. They were converging rapidly, lances ready, towards each other and Danny knew that Jayden would win but he didn't slow down.

And she would've won; if it hadn't been for the eye visor on her helmet. The bouncing from the horse's galloping made the visor come loose and it slammed shut on her. A newly blinded Jayden fumbled with the visor and as she did, she lost her grip on the lance and it fell to the ground. Jayden continued the course despite her predicament.

Jayden continued to work on her helmet but it was too late. She opened her helmet just in time to see Danny's lance smash into her armor. The wooden weapon splintered into hundreds of pieces and the blow ripped Jayden from her horse then she hit the ground; her armor clanked as she bumped around inside it.

Danny's horse slowed to a stop and Danny lifted his own visor. He looked at the motionless makeshift knight and exclaimed proudly, "Is there any sport that I'm *not* good at?"

*****

Sarita was at a location that she knew far too well: detention. You see, although Sarita was an above average student and a star athlete, she was also very opinionated and stubborn. It was these characteristics, along with her habit of speaking out of turn, that landed her in trouble.

"How nice of you to join us, Sarita." Commented a familiar voice from inside the room. It was none other than Staci. Apparently, she was the detention teacher. "Please, have a seat." Staci offered and two arm restraints latched onto Sarita and pulled her to the only chair in the white room. The chair strapped her legs down and her arms; rendering Sarita completely immobile.

"This is the part where you torture me to death, huh?" Sarita asked, unafraid.

"Torture you? Yes. To death? No. I don't need to kill you. I'm sure that my associates are about to do one of your friends in as we speak-"

"They're your friends too. Or…at least they used to be." Sarita interrupted.

"It's irrelevant. Your team will lose and I won't have to lift a finger."

Staci stood from the teacher's desk and pulled down a blank projector screen from the ceiling. "While I have you here though," Staci continued, "I'd like to show you a slideshow that I've prepared; a compilation of all your failures. The entire slideshow is meant to remind you of every time you lost to me." Sarita rolled her eyes and cursed under her breath. "What was that?!" Staci snapped.

"I said have an *itch*." Sarita lied.

"Sure. Whatever." Staci clicked play and sat back in her chair. On her desk, there was a crust less sandwich, sliced diagonally and a soda. She grabbed a half of the sandwich and took a bite. "Let's begin with first grade." She said between chews.

Seconds changed to minutes. Minutes became hours. And the slideshow dragged on. Sarita started to wish Staci would just kill her. Finally, after what felt like years, the show came to an end.

"That's weird. I was sure you'd be in Limbo by now…I guess I'll go look for more photos of you sucking at life. Don't go anywhere." Staci joked as she left the room.

"'Don't go anywhere.'" Sarita mocked under her breath.

I gotta get outta here, Sarita thought. She knew this all had to be an illusion created by Staci, no doubt, but she needed an exit. And then it hit her. Staci couldn't possibly maintain an illusion if she was unconscious. *What am I thinking? These cuffs are too tight. I'll never get free to knock Staci out,* she reasoned. But a few moments later Sarita had the solution.

Sarita listened intently for signs of Staci's return. When she knew the coast was clear, Sarita sprouted vines that were shaped like hands from her palms and the two leaf appendages stretched across the room to the teacher's desk. Their target: the second half of Staci's sandwich.

The green hands retrieved the sandwich and placed it on Sarita's desk. Using the left hand to lift the top layer of bread and the right hand to hold the bottom half down, Sarita split the sandwich and then did something very unladylike: she snorted and spit right in Staci's sandwich.

The substitute hands closed the sandwich and replaced in on Staci's desk only seconds before Staci walked back in.

"I found a few yearbooks that have really bad pictures of you in them. That'll have to do." She said as she entered the room.

"Fine, but before we do, can I finish your sandwich? I'm starving. Like hardcore."

Staci looked over at the sandwich on the desk. She placed the yearbooks down and picked the sandwich up.

"This sandwich?" Staci asked. Sarita nodded. Staci smiled and took a huge bite. "This sandwich that I'm eating?"

"Yes. That one…" said Sarita, faking disappointment.

"Oh. I'm sor-" Staci passed out cold, mid-sentence and collapsed on the floor. That wasn't regular saliva and mucus Sarita spit into the sandwich. It was a mixture of a highly concentrated sleep-inducing agent. She invented it herself.

The chair released Sarita instantly and she headed over to Staci. All around, the walls began to fade away and the grassy meadow could be seen again. Sarita stood over the sleeping girl and shook her head.

"The Staci I knew wouldn't have fallen for such an obvious trap." She remarked.

Back at the meadow, everyone else's illusions had ended and, so far, the Phalanx had won every fight. There was only one pair still battling...

*****

Chris was so happy to be on land that he kissed the ground when the hallucination disappeared. In his alternate reality, he and Laura were skydiving and since Laura had control over wind, Chris had been at a severe disadvantage. But the ball was in his court now...and he didn't want to play anymore.

"Laura," He began, "I'm not going to fight you. I would never lay a hand on you because I love you too much for that. So, do what you want with me. I won't fight back."

Laura paused for a minute as if she was thinking it over then said, "As you wish."

Laura summoned a gale force wind that whipped Chris into a nearby tree but when he hit it, he temporarily lost control of his powers and a spike launched from Chris's chest.

The spike headed straight for Laura and enlodged itself in her abdomen. Her shirt dripped red with her own life fluid and the tip of the projectile protruded from her back. A single drop of blood rolled down to the tip of the skewer then descended to the ground and landed, gently, on a blade of grass...

Chapter 11

"Devastation"

Devastation: To bring to ruin; to reduce to chaos or helpless-

ness

Tears trickled down Laura's face as she dropped to her knees, silently. Chris sprinted to assist Laura while the rest of us watched in horror. Even Derrick has a shocked expression on his face.

Chris delicately cradled Laura's head in his lap as he wiped her tears away; completely neglecting his own tears. Laura smiled weakly at her boyfriend. She was herself again. Derrick's mind control had been lifted somehow. Chris began to bawl uncontrollably at the sight of her smile.

"I've never seen you so emotional," Laura said feebly, "It's refreshing." Chris smiled to hide the pain and turned his attention to the spike in her stomach. He considered pulling it out, but he knew it was the only thing keeping her alive. Laura grabbed Chris' hand and they interlocked fingers. "I could hear you-" Laura started then coughed roughly and continued. "I heard every word. It was the sweetest thing anyone has ever said to me."

"I'm so sorry, Laura. I never meant for this to happen."

"Shh," Laura cut him off. "Don't beat yourself up over this. I don't blame you. Not at all." Laura breathed in sharply. "I love you, Chris."

"I love you too..." He whispered back. Chris leaned in for one last kiss and moments later, Laura passed away.

Everyone was speechless and in tears except for X and Derrick who just looked stunned. Derrick's Sapphire Star medallion began to radiate brightly then disappeared from around his neck and reappeared around Xavier's. Then, without warning, Derrick, Staci, Jayden, Curt and Jared dematerialized into sand and were sucked into space. Even Laura's inanimate body changed and vanished; leaving Chris clutching air.

"Well done, guys," X broke the silence, "That was much more graphic that I foresaw but-" Xavier's words obviously struck a nerve with Chris, because he stood up, clothes stained with Laura's blood, and got in X's face. Chris' blood shot eyes told the story of a broken man.

"Did you just say that you knew this would happen?" Chris' lips trembled as he spoke. "Are you saying you could've prevented Laura from *dying* in my arms?!" Chris was on the verge of losing it.

Chris' unstable condition made Xavier uneasy and, when he answered Chris, X was kinda stuttering. "W-Well, yes. But it n-needed to happen for us to be v-victorious-" Chris punched X square in the face, possibly breaking his nose, before he could finish sentence. X tumbled backward and Chris walked away without a word.

The remaining four of us were so appalled by X as a whole that we abandoned the meadow as well; leaving Xavier alone to tend his own wounds.

*****

Back at Brody's house, there was another meeting. Only this time, a different person was leading. The mysterious stranger was now in charge (he told them to call him Mr. L).

"Ok. Brody. Report. Did Frankie get my message and the package for his friend?" the man asked.

"Yes sir. I delivered it during the Remington Estate fire." Brody answered.

"Excellent work. Carrie?" Mr. L said.

"Huh?" responded a startled Carrie. She had been listening to her mp3 player the whole time.

"What is Frankie's current status?" Mr. L inquired.

"Umm..." Carrie fumbled around in her purse for the notes she had scribbled down. "Ah. Here we go. Frankie and his little group or whatever just beat Derrick's group. Also, his friend Laura died. And...I think that's it."

Mr. L seemed concerned by the news. Around his neck, there were three medallions: a diamond sphere, a maroon triangle, and a crimson rhombus. He adjusted these medallions as he pondered his next move.

Mr. L sighed. "This was an unexpected obstacle. I must go. I have some business to take care of. Don't wait for me. I could be gone for a while."

And before anyone could object, Mr. L was out the door. Rick, Alexis, Timmy, Carrie and Brody all shared the same confused look.

"What do we do until then?" Alexis wondered.

Everyone just shrugged in response.

*****

Meanwhile, in a distant laboratory, an archaeologist was deciphering a message written in hieroglyphics that she discovered during her last visit to Cairo. The woman couldn't have been older than 22 or 23, with olive skin and high cheekbones. She wasn't very tall, (only 5'1) and she had an average figure a woman her height. The archeologist had her hair pulled back and wore a white lab coat with a name badge that said Dr. Elizabeth Bronson.

Dr. Bronson removed her glasses when she finally interpreted the message's meaning. It was a warning; a prophecy that foretold of an impending apocalypse that would occur on the tenth month of the third year of the Tsol Battle Championship. She had no idea what that was but the hieroglyphics gave a name of someone she thought could explain a few things.

I need to find this Xavier Gonzalez before it's too late, she thought.

*****

Mr. L didn't return for three whole months and when he did, it wasn't Brody he had come to see.

*****

I awoke that morning to a pounding sound at my front door that shook me from my slumber.

"What day is it?" I asked aloud even though I knew exactly what day it was. It was my 16th birthday, but I was in no mood to celebrate. In the past few months, I gained superpowers, my two best friends turned out to be aliens, (one of which was evil and the other was just plain crazy) I was trapped in a burning building, and my evil alien best friend and a handful of my other friends vanished into thin air. Not to mention my friend Laura died and my friend Chris feels so responsible that he secluded himself off somewhere and no one can find him. Things couldn't possibly get any worse.

On my dresser drawer, there was a note. It read:

HAPPY 16TH BIRTHDAY, SWEETIE!!! When I get home from work, we're going to dinner to celebrate my little man's big 1-6. Just me, you and David.
Love you, Mommy.

Indifferent to the note, I made my way downstairs to see what was so important that someone felt the need to beat down my door.

When I opened the door, there was a black guy standing on the porch. He stood at about 5'11. The man had a mildly muscular build with a strong face and bold facial features. He wore a tight black t-shirt and blue jeans. But most importantly, he had three medallions around his neck: a diamond sphere, a maroon triangle, and a crimson rhombus. It was Mr. L but I knew him by a different name.

"Dad?" I asked, with a huge, cheesy grin.

"Frankie," My dad smiled back, then pulled a pistol from the small of his back, cocked it and pressed the barrel between my eyes. The cold steel on my face sent a chill down my spine and my smile faded. "Happy 16th Birthday, son."

I take back what I said earlier. *Now* things couldn't possibly get any worse…

Here's a Sneak Peek at the second book in the Star Struck Trilogy:

Star Struck
Transition

The Prologue

The cargo hold of the plane was the first to go. Its doors were rattling uncontrollably then they flew off the hinges.

The fuel tank ruptured next; spilling gasoline like rain to the land below. The left wing's turbine engines exploded suddenly, sending the aircraft plummeting from the sky. The pilot and co-pilot were dead and the passengers onboard were screaming, crying and hyperventilating. The oxygen masks dropped down from the compartments but everyone was too panicked to utilize them.

A handful of hysterical passengers wedged the fuselage door open and jumped out, hoping to die of a heart attack before they hit the ground. It was pure chaos onboard and I couldn't focus. My friend Kyle and I waded through the madness to cockpit. Neither of us knew how to land a plane but we had to try something.

Autopilot was disabled and there were too many buttons to B.S. our way through. The plane's altimeter showed that we were dropping hundreds of feet per second. It was hopeless; we were going to crash.

"Why, Kyle?" I asked my friend. "Why did you do it? You've doomed us all, you realize that, right?"

"I'm sorry, Franklin. I lost control." He replied.

The right wing was ripped from the plane and we entered a downward freefall. Kyle and I were snatched from the cockpit, pulled to the back of the plane and pinned to the wall. The passengers were frozen with fear because they knew what was coming. And as they all prayed for their lives to be spared, I began longing for simpler times. Like a few months ago when I was standing at my front doorstep, on my birthday, with a gun to my head and my father as the wielder of the weapon. Ah. Those were the days...

.